"You're...not staying here?" Campion asked nervously

Guy's eyebrows rose. "Of course I am. Where else would I stay?"

"Well, all right, you can stay," Campion said, "but I'm not staying in this cottage with you." She headed for the door, but was brought to an abrupt halt as he swung her off her feet and deposited her on the floor again with such force that her teeth rattled.

"Now, let's get one thing straight," he told her savagely, all pretense of calm good humor stripped from him. "I've given my word, both professionally and personally, that your manuscript will be delivered on time. I've laid myself on the line for you and your damn book, Campion, and no matter what it takes, you are going to deliver."

No matter what it takes... Campion shivered.

1 0696854

PENNY JORDAN was constantly in trouble in school because of her inability to stop daydreaming—especially during French lessons. In her teens she was an avid romance reader, although it didn't occur to her to try writing one herself until she was older. "My first half-dozen attempts ended up ingloriously," she remembers, "but I persevered, and one manuscript was finished." She plucked up the courage to send it to a publisher, convinced her book would be rejected. It wasn't, and the rest is history! Penny is married and lives in Cheshire.

Books by Penny Jordan

HARLEQUIN PRESENTS

HARLEQUIN SIGNATURE EDITION

Don't miss any of our special offers. Write to us at the following address for information on our newest releases.

Harlequin Reader Service
901 Fuhrmann Blvd., P.O. Box 1397, Buffalo, NY 14240
Canadian address: P.O. Box 603,
Fort Erie, Ont. L2A 5X3

PENNY JORDAN

JORDAN

force of feeling

Harlequin Books

TORONTO • NEW YORK • LONDON
AMSTERDAM • PARIS • SYDNEY • HAMBURG
STOCKHOLM • ATHENS • TOKYO • MILAN

Harlequin Presents first edition May 1989
ISBN 0-373-11169-X

Original hardcover edition published in 1988
by Mills & Boon Limited

Copyright © 1988 by Penny Jordan. All rights reserved.
Except for use in any review, the reproduction or utilization
of this work in whole or in part in any form by any electronic,
mechanical or other means, now known or hereafter invented,
including xerography, photocopying and recording,
or in any information storage or retrieval system, is forbidden without
the permission of the publisher, Harlequin Enterprises Limited,
225 Duncan Mill Road, Don Mills, Ontario, Canada M3B 3K9.

All the characters in this book have no existence outside the
imagination of the author and have no relation whatsoever to
anyone bearing the same name or names. They are not even
distantly inspired by any individual known or unknown to the
author, and all incidents are pure invention.

® are Trademarks registered in the United States Patent and
Trademark Office and in other countries.

Printed in U.S.A.

CHAPTER ONE

As SHE stepped out into the busy London street and flagged down a passing taxi, Campion glanced irritably at her watch. She was going to be late for lunch, but luckily she knew that Lucy would wait for her.

How relaxing it must be to be the adored wife of a wealthy businessman, with all the time in the world at one's disposal and no pressures besetting one at all, other than the need to look beautiful and give good dinner parties. And then she chided herself for being unfair. Lucy was not just a beautiful woman, she was an intelligent one as well. It was having to deal with Guy French that had made her feel like this. She had never liked the man, and when her agent had first gone into partnership with him, she had warned her then that she wanted nothing to do with him.

Helena had been openly astonished.

'But, Campion, my dear, he's the best in the business,' she had told her. 'The deals he gets for his authors . . .'

'He's not my type, Helena. I don't like the man, and I don't like his methods of business.' Nor his morals, she had wanted to add, but she had kept that bit back. Now, having confronted him face to face, she realised that she had been quite right to protest. She didn't like him.

Nor had she liked what he had had to say about her new manuscript.

She scowled ferociously to herself, causing the taxi driver to grimace slightly as he caught sight of her expression in his rear-view mirror.

She could have been very attractive; she had a good body, tall with long legs—he had noticed those as she'd got into his cab—and full, high breasts, even though she had chosen to drape herself in what looked like several layers of the same drab, beige fabric, which did nothing for her pale English skin, nor for her fair hair. And fancy wearing it like that! She had it scraped back tightly into a large French pleat, a style which privately he thought did very little for any woman. If she had chosen to wear it in one of the many attractive styles favoured by the new Duchess of York, now . . .

He stopped outside a smart Kensington restaurant, wondering what on earth this unmade-up, rather tired-looking woman was doing lunching in such an 'in' place. She paid the bill and tipped him well. She had nice hands, he noticed, with long, tapering fingers, but her nails were cut short and unpolished.

But, oddly enough, he noticed as she walked away from him that she was wearing perfume. Strange, that . . . In his experience, most women only wore perfume for a man.

Perhaps she was some sort of odd 'Kiss-o-gram' girl, and underneath those drab clothes . . . Whistling to himself as he let his imagination run riot, he drove off.

Campion, with no idea of what was going on inside his head, walked angrily into the restaurant. The perfume the sales girl had sprayed all over her as she had rushed through Harvey Nichols earlier in the morning still clung to her skin. Normally she didn't like anything the slightest bit scented, but this was rather pleasant, old-fashioned and faintly evocative of a summer garden, heavy with the scent of roses.

For once she was oblivious to the amused glances she collected as she wove her way through the crowded tables full of other diners. They were women, in the main, smartly dressed and made up, all of them paying more attention to their fellow lunchers than to the skimpy food on their plates. After all, that was what they were really paying for, to see and be seen.

At last Campion spotted Lucy. She was sitting at a table for two, in what Campion suspected was the best part of the restaurant.

She was dressed in blue, a soft, pretty, lavender blue that suited her fair skin and dark hair and, as always when she saw her, Campion was struck anew by her friend's loveliness.

They had been at school together, and then at university, but no one had been surprised when Lucy had married almost immediately upon leaving Oxford. The man she had married had once been her boss, but not for long.

'Sorry I'm late,' Campion apologised, as she sat down and took the menu proffered by the waiter.

'Problems?' Lucy asked sympathetically.

Campion made a face. 'Is it so obvious? Helena's not well, and I'm having to deal with Guy French,' she frowned, aware that there was a good deal that she was keeping back.

Lucy plainly felt it too, because she pressed lightly, 'And?'

'And he's querying several points in my new book.

I've been working to a deadline on it as it is . . .'

Lucy knew all about the book in question. Campion had been a successful writer of historical fiction in a modest way for almost three years, but some time previously, with the encouragement of Helena, and backed by a large publishing firm, she had agreed to attempt to produce something a little more commercial than her usual skilful and very factual blend of historical fact and fiction.

At first, she had been thrilled with the commission. It would give her something to get her teeth into, something with a much broader scope than her usual books, but that had been before she realised what the publishers truly wanted of her. Now she was locked into a contract that demanded that the manuscript be finished and soon, and the changes Guy French was demanding . . .

She was not that naïve, no matter what he might think, and she had been well aware that she was expected to provide a certain sexual content to her book. Previously her books had dealt more with the historical than the personal aspect of her characters' lives, but this time . . . This time her heroine, the Lady Lynsey de Frères, as a very rich ward of court, and therefore a valuable pawn in the hands of Henry the Eighth, would be expected by her readers to do more than simply acquiesce to the marriage arranged for her by Henry.

And the problem was that she knew in her heart of hearts that Guy was right.

He wanted her to be more explicit in her descriptions of the morals and manners of the times—much, much more explicit. He had even pointed out to her that the publishers had already rejected her first manuscript on the grounds that the heroine was too insipid and unreal to hold their readers' interest. And now she was running out of time, and Helena would not be back at work for another whole month, a full week after her final manuscript was due on her publishers' desk.

If she tried to cancel the contract now, the publishers would be legally free to sue her and, although she did not think they would do that, it would be a very black mark against her.

Where had it all gone wrong? She had been so thrilled with the original commission, and now . . .

'What does Guy suggest you do?' Lucy pressed her.

'He wants me to have a secretary.' She scowled again, as she had done in the taxi.

'Well, what's wrong with that?' Lucy asked her, plainly at a loss to understand her reluctance. 'I've thought for some time that you could do with one. You type your own manuscripts, and it must be very time-consuming . . .'

It was, but that was the way she preferred it. To Campion, writing was a very personal thing indeed, so personal that on some occasions she could almost feel that *she* was the character she was writing about, and on those occasions she didn't want to have someone else with her, watching her, monitoring her reactions. It would make her feel so vulnerable, so . . . She gave a little shiver, her eyes unknowingly registering her fear.

She had lovely eyes, Lucy thought, watching her compassionately: neither green nor blue, but something in between. With a little care and thought, she could have been a very beautiful woman. They were the same age—twenty-six—and yet at a first glance Campion could have been mistaken for someone easily ten years older. Lucy itched to take charge of her—to make her throw away her hideously drab clothes, to do her face, and to get her to have her hair properly styled.

Her husband, an acute and very shrewd man, had said to her the first time she introduced him to Campion, 'What happened to her? She's like a plant that's been blighted by frost.'

'A man,' Lucy had told him carefully. Because, after all, the story was Campion's and not her own, and she knew how much her friend hated talking about Craig.

'I don't *want* a secretary!' Campion exploded now. 'I just want to be left alone to get on with my work.'

'Well, *tell* Guy that,' Lucy suggested reasonably.

'I have, and he won't listen. He's insisting that I must have someone to work for me. It's almost as though he thinks I need a gaoler, someone to keep me at work. And then there's this tour coming up,' she added angrily.

'Tour?'

'Oh, you remember. I told you about it. A small publicity tour for that book I did about Cornwall. Guy seems to think that if I can have a secretary, I can somehow manage to dictate huge chunks of the new book in between signing sessions, and she can then presumably type them up while I'm signing.'

Lucy sighed and reached out across the table to take her hand. 'Campion, be honest, if Helena had suggested this, and not Guy, would you feel quite so strongly?'

Campion frowned and then admitted huskily, 'I don't know. There's something about him that rubs me up the wrong way. I feel as edgy as a cat walking on too hot sand whenever he comes near me . . .' She rubbed tiredly at her eyes. 'I don't like him,' she added childishly, 'but I don't know why I react so strongly to him.'

I do, Lucy thought achingly, and it's called sexual awareness, but she knew that there was no way she could say that to Campion.

Instead, she asked carefully, 'So what do you intend to do?'

'What *can* I do?' Campion asked her bitterly, revealing how much she resented what was happening to her. 'I have to go along with what Guy's saying. I don't have any option. Do you know what he told me?' She took a deep breath, fighting for self-control as she leaned across the table, her eyes flashing fiercely, 'He actually admitted that *he* was the one who advised the publishers to reject my first draft. He had the utter gall to tell me that he thought it wasn't worthy of me—that he had seen more emotion in the writings of a seven-year-old! He told me my book was flat and boring, and that my characters, especially Lynsey, had about as much reality as cardboard cut-outs!' Suddenly the fight left her and her eyes dulled. 'And the worst thing is that I know he's right. Oh, God, Lucy, why on earth did I ever take on this commission?'

'Because it's giving you an opportunity to stretch yourself,' Lucy reminded her gently. 'You wanted to do it, Campion,' she told her.

Opposite her, Campion groaned. 'Don't remind me. I must have been mad! I can't do it, Lucy. I know that I can't.'

'Have you told Guy this?'

Immediately her eyes darkened with anger.

'Throw myself on his mercy? Never!'

'Then what are you going to do?'

'Get back to work—not here in London. Helena has a small cottage she lets her writers use. I'm going to go there . . . that way, Guy won't be able to force me to have a secretary,' she added childishly. 'I'm going tonight. It's in Pembroke.'

'*Wales,* at this time of the year?' Lucy shuddered. 'We're already into November . . . Which reminds me, have you any plans for Christmas? Howard and I will be going to Dorset as usual, and of course we'd love you to join us.'

Lucy had inherited, from her grandfather, a very lovely small manor house in Dorset, and she and Howard spent every Christmas there, and as much time as they could during the rest of the year.

'Please do,' she coaxed. 'I'm going to need your help this year. I think I'm pregnant.'

Shortly after their marriage Lucy had suffered a very traumatic miscarriage, and since then Howard had flatly refused to even consider the idea of them trying for another child, but now it seemed he had relented.

'Dr Harrison has finally persuaded Howard that what happened before won't happen again, and I'm giving you fair warning here and now that I'm going to ask you to be godmother.'

Just after three, they left the restaurant, Lucy to go shopping and Campion to go back to her flat to pack for her trip to Wales.

She had been to Helena's cottage several times before, but never to work, only as a visitor. She had never before needed the solitude it offered. Writing had always come so easily to her—*writing* still did, it was the *emotions* of her characters she was having problems with.

She packed carefully and frugally: a couple of pairs of jeans, seldom worn these days, but they would still fit her, plenty of bulky sweaters, and a set of thermal underwear, just in case. Some socks, her portable typewriter, just in case the generator broke down and the electric machine Helena had installed at the cottage didn't work.

She would need wellingtons, she reminded herself; she would have to buy some before she left. And food, which meant a trip to her local supermarket. Plenty of typing paper, her notes—the list was endless, and all the time she was getting ready her conversation with Guy French kept going round and round in her mind.

He had the reputation of having a very acid tongue, but he had never used it on her. And yet, this morning, he had virtually torn her apart with what he had said; all of it in that calm, even, logical voice of his, which stated his assembled facts as though they were incontrovertible truths. And the worst of it was that they very probably were. Her heroine *did* lack emotional depth. Campion sat down wearily, too tired to hide from the truth any longer. She had no idea what she was going to do about Lynsey.

When she had tried to deflect Guy, by reminding him that her heroine was a young girl of sixteen, he had calmly countered by saying that in that age girls of sixteen were often wives and mothers and that, since she herself had described her heroine as being spirited and passionate, couldn't she see that it just wasn't in character for her to calmly accept King Henry's edict that she marry a man she had never seen before, especially not when, according to his notes, she had already hinted that Lynsey considered herself to be in love with her cousin?

'Wouldn't she at least have tried to see Francis? Think of it—a beautiful young girl of sixteen, rich and wilful, condemned by the King's will to marry a man to whom he owes a favour, a man moreover who has the reputation of procuring for that same king women with whom he amuses himself behind his wife's back. Surely she would be angry and disgusted at such a proposed marriage? Surely she would be desperate enough to make a rash attempt to stop it? Allowing herself to be compromised by another man would be one way. And surely she would choose that man to be her cousin, the boy whom she thinks she loves?'

It all made sense, but for some reason Campion just could not breathe life into her heroine. She just could not even mentally visualise Lynsey doing what Guy suggested, even though she knew what he was saying was perfectly true.

She had told him as much, adding defiantly that the publishers could sue her if they wished, but she was not going to change a word of her manuscript.

He had looked at her then, his grey eyes focusing on her and turning smokily dark.

For a moment she had actually expected him to get up from behind his desk and seize hold of her and shake her. No small task, even for a man of his height and build, because she was well over five foot eight and, despite her fragile frame, no lightweight either. But instead he had controlled himself and said icily, 'Quitting, Campion? You surprise me. What is it you're so afraid of?'

'Nothing. I'm not afraid of anything,' she had flung at him, and somehow, before she knew where she was, he had tricked her into committing herself to the re-writes.

And now she had to do them. But *her* way, and not his—and without a secretary.

All this burning of adrenalin had left her feeling oddly tired. She looked at her watch. An hour's sleep before she left would do her good. Sleep was something that often evaded her during the night, and she had to take brief catnaps during the day whenever she could.

She went into her bedroom and closed the curtains.

Her flat was as drab as her clothes, furnished mainly in beiges and browns, colours bordering on nothingness.

She undressed, wrapped herself in a towelling robe and lay on her bed but, irritatingly, exhausted though she was, sleep would not come. Instead a multitude of jumbled images flashed repeatedly across her brain.

Guy French, tall, and dark-haired; a man she had heard other women describe admiringly as sexually devastating. Perhaps, but not to her, never to her . . .

Her mind switched to Lucy. How long had they known one another? They had started at boarding-school together, two small, pigtailed girls in brand new uniforms, both wanting desperately to cry and neither feeling they should.

They had been friends a long time. Lucy's new circle of friends, those she had made through Howard, looked askance at Campion, probably wondering what she and pretty, glamorous Lucy had in common.

She wondered if Lucy had told Howard about

her. Probably, they had that sort of relationship, and Howard was the kind of man who invited one's trust. How lucky Lucy had been in her marriage! How wise to wait a little while and not to allow herself to be swept off her feet in the first rapture of physical desire, as *she* had been . . .

As she had been . . . How impossible that seemed now! Now, she could no more imagine the deep frozen heart of hers being melted than she could imagine flying to the moon. Both were impossible.

Once, a long time ago, things had been different, she had been different.

Once, she had known what it felt like to have her whole body surge with joy at a man's touch, almost at the sound of his voice, but that had been before . . .

She gave a deep sigh and opened her eyes, but it was no use, for some reason, the past was crowding in on her today.

For some reason? She knew the reason well enough: it had been the look in Guy's eyes when he had asked her in that even, calm voice of his if she actually knew what it was like to feel emotion. She had felt as though her very soul had been raked with red-hot irons, but she had kept her expression cool and unrevealing. Let him think what he liked, just as long as he never guessed the truth.

The truth. Her mouth twisted bitterly. How melodramatic that sounded now! And what was it, really?

She closed her eyes again and tried to focus her concentration on her book, on Lynsey, but it was virtually impossible. Guy's dark face surfaced through the barriers of her will, and then another male face, equally dark-haired, equally good-looking, but younger, shallower . . . weaker, she recognised.

She had been nineteen when she'd met Craig, and a rather naïve nineteen at that. Her girls' school had been sheltered; she was an only child, with wealthy parents who spent a good deal of their time out of the country, and consequently she had spent very little time with them until she left school. And in that long, hot summer before she started at Oxford she had felt uncomfortable with them, alien and alone, and had wished that she had given in to Lucy's plea to accept an invitation from her parents to spend the summer with them in the South of France.

Instead she had mooned about at home, sensing her parents' inability to understand her, feeling unacceptable to her local peers, with whom she seemed to have little in common. And then she had met Craig.

He had come to the house to see her father about something, she couldn't remember what. Her parents had been out and she had been sunbathing in the garden. She had been flattered by the admiring way he had looked at her bikini-clad body. He had remarked on that and she had offered him a drink.

One drink had turned into two, and in the end he had spent most of the afternoon in the garden with her.

Even then she had sensed a restlessness about him, a yearning—a desperation almost, but she had put it down to the same malaise she suffered herself, too naïve to recognise then their basic differences.

He had asked her out, to a local tennis-club

dance. At first her parents had been pleased that
she was making friends, and then her father had
cautioned her against getting too involved.

She had known by then about Craig's background: about the father who drank and the
mother who struggled to bring up her five children.
She had also learned about Craig's bitterness at not
being able to take up the free scholarship he had
won, because of lack of money. Her father had
told her bluntly that Craig had a chip on his
shoulder, but she had refused to listen to him. By
this time, she was in love.

Or so she thought.

Her mouth twisted bitterly. She ought to have
listened to her father, but she had thought she
knew better. She had thought that Craig loved her,
when in reality what he had loved was her parents'
wealth and social standing.

As the summer had deepened, so had her
feelings. He had known exactly how to arouse her,
how to make her ache and yearn for the final act of
possession. Even now, remembering, her flesh
remained cold and unmoving, her mind unable to
really comprehend how she could have felt that
way; but she had.

— They had made love for the first time in an
idyllic setting: a small, enclosed glade in a local
wood, a privately owned lane, in actual fact, but
with an absentee landlord. Ostensibly, they had
gone on a picnic. Craig had brought a blanket,
plaid and soft, and very new. Where had he got the
money from to buy it? she wondered now.
Certainly not from the job he had told her he had,
working for a local accountant as a trainee.

He had made love to her with need and passion,

or so she had thought, but there had been none of the rapture she had imagined in the ultimate act of possession, and she had rather disliked the heavy sensation of him lying over her afterwards. She had gone home feeling faintly disappointed, until she remembered girls at school saying that the first time was not always very good.

It had been Craig who had first brought up the subject of marriage. What if she were to be pregnant? he had asked her. It could have happened. And because she was genuinely afraid, and because in her innocence she thought that, since they had been lovers, they must love one another, and because she was lonely and desperately in need of someone of her own, she had listened.

No, she had done more than listen. She had married him. Quietly and secretly, one month after he had first made love to her. Her parents were away at the time.

The newly-weds had been waiting for them when they returned.

Campion struggled to sit up, her throat suddenly tight with tension, her breathing shallow.

She would never forget the scene that followed, nor Craig's fury when he realised that her father was not prepared to either settle a large sum of money on her, or to support them.

To see him change in front of her eyes, from someone she thought loved her to someone who had married her purely and simply for financial gain, had been too much of a shock for her to take in. She had tried to plead with him, to remind him that even without money they still had one another, and he had turned on her then, his face livid with rage.

'For Christ's sake!' he had said. 'Do you think I

would have married you if it hadn't been for who
you are?'

'You—you said you loved me,' she had
stammered, unable to understand his abrupt change
of character.

'And you fell for it, didn't you, you stupid little
bitch!' he had snarled at her. 'Like taking candy
from a baby—only it seems that your daddy isn't
going to play along. Well, I'd better get something
out of this, otherwise the whole village is going to
hear about how easily I got little Miss Goody-two-
shoes here into bed, Mr Roberts,' he had challenged
her father.

She had cried out then, but he had turned on her,
his expression vicious, quite definitely not good-
looking any more.

'I should have made sure that you were pregnant,
shouldn't I?'

And he had gone on to make such derogatory
remarks about her sexuality that she hadn't been able
to take in all the insults he was hurling at her—not
then.

The marriage had been annulled—her father had
seen to that, but somehow Campion had felt as
though she were encased in ice. She had gone on to
Oxford, but she had gone there a changed person.
Lucy noticed it and asked her what was wrong, and
she had broken down and confided in her friend.
That had been the last time she cried. The shock of
what had happened wore off, but the humiliation
remained. Whenever a man approached her, she
froze him off, and gradually she got the reputation of
being withdrawn and sexually frigid. She hadn't
cared. She was never going to let a man get

emotionally or physically close to her ever again. Craig had held up for her such an image of herself that it had destroyed totally her awakening sexuality. Whenever she remembered how innocently and joyously she had abandoned herself to him, her skin crawled with self-loathing; gradually, she withdrew further and further into herself.

Then her parents were killed in an outbreak of hostilities in Beirut when they were there on business. She had sold the house and bought herself her small flat. The rest of the money she had donated to various charities.

No man would ever again be tempted to make love to her because he thought she could be his ticket to rich living.

Over the years, Lucy had tried to coax her to change, to dress more attractively, to meet other men, but she had always refused. What was the point? She didn't want a man in her life in any capacity, and what man would want *her?*

As Craig had already told her, her only attraction lay in her father's wealth; he had wanted her for that alone. Making love to her had been a necessity, a means to an end, and he had let her know in no uncertain terms just how lacking in pleasure he had found their coming together.

She actually flinched now as she remembered his insults. Her father had tried to stop him, she remembered tiredly. And, afterwards, her parents had both tried to offer her some comfort. They had never criticised or condemned her; she had done that for herself. They had tried to reach her, but the gap between them was too deep. They had never been a close family, and now she was too hurt and bitter to accept their pity, and so she had buried her pain away deep down inside herself where no one could see it.

Why couldn't she use those memories of how Craig had made her feel to flesh out the character of Lynsey?

She knew why. It was because they had been so false, so dangerously deceptive, and as for the physical pleasure of Craig's lovemaking . . . There had been none in his possession, and she cringed from the memory of it, knowing that here again the lack had been hers.

She flinched again as she recalled Guy French's last words to her this morning.

'Perhaps you'd have been better off casting your heroine as a nun, Campion,' he had drawled mockingly. 'Because it seems that that's the way you want her to live.'

She had left the office while she still had some measure of control. She had been tempted to tear up her manuscript in front of his eyes; in fact, when she thought about it now, she was surprised by the violence of her reaction. She shivered slightly and got up. She wasn't going to sleep, so there was no point in lying here thinking about things that could not be changed.

It was almost six o'clock, and she still had to go to the supermarket. It was a long drive to Pembroke . . . She almost decided to delay her departure until the morning but, if she did, Guy French would probably be on the telephone, telling her he had already found her a secretary. He was that kind of man. No, she needed to leave now, while there was still time.

While there was still time . . . She frowned a little at her own mental choice of words. It was almost as though she was frightened of the man; almost as though, in some way, she found him threatening. She shrugged the thought aside. Guy French was a bully; she had never liked him and she never would.

The media considered him to be the glamour boy of publishing, although at thirty-five he hardly qualified for the term 'boy', she told herself scathingly. He represented everything male that she detested: good looks, charm, and that appallingly apparent raw sexuality that other women seemed to find so attractive, and which she found physically repellant.

She had seen his eyes narrow slightly this morning as he came to greet her, and she had instinctively stepped back from him. He hadn't touched her, letting his hand fall to his side, but she had still flushed darkly, all too conscious of his amusement and contempt.

No doubt to a man like him she was just a joke: a physically unattractive woman with whom he was forced to deal because it was part of his job. She had seen too many men look at her and then look away to be under any illusions. She wasn't like Lucy—pretty, confident. Craig had destroyed for her for ever any belief she might once have had that she had any claim to feminine beauty. Ugly, sexless—that was how he had described her in that cruel, taunting voice of his, and that was how she saw herself, and how she believed others saw her as well.

But there were other things in life that brought pleasure, apart from love. She had found that pleasure in her work. *Had* found . . . Until Guy French had started tearing her novel apart, and with it her self-confidence.

That was what really hurt, she admitted—knowing that he was right when he described her characters as unanimated and without depth. But she had been

commissioned to write a historical novel with a
factual background, not a love story dressed up in
period costume.

She could, of course, always back down and
admit defeat; she could tell Guy French to inform
the publishers that she was backing out of the
contract. They wouldn't sue her she felt sure and
with withdrawal would stop Guy from hounding
her. There were other books she could write . . .
Moodily, she stared out of the window. Her flat
was one of several in a small, anonymous, purpose-
built block, with nothing to distinguish it from its
fellows. Once, as teenagers, she and Lucy had
talked of the lives they would lead as adults, of the
homes they would have. She remembered quite
sharply telling Lucy that she would fill hers with
fresh flowers, full of colour and scent.

Fresh flowers! It had been years since she had
last bought any . . . the wreath for her parents'
funeral.

Impatient with herself, Campion went to get her
coat and her car keys, and then headed for her
local supermarket.

CHAPTER TWO

SHE must have been mad to have attempted this long journey so late in the evening, Campion admitted bitterly as she stared out into the dark night.

Somehow, out here in the middle of Wales, the darkness seemed so much more intense than it had in London. Almost it felt as though it was pressing in on her, surrounding her. She shivered despite the warmth inside the car, wondering why it was she should be so much more aware of the fact that it was late November, and the weather wet and cold and very inhospitable, than she had been when she had first left.

Perhaps because when she'd left her mind had been full of Guy French, and how angry he would be when he found that she had escaped.

So he thought he could force her to complete the book by taking on a secretary, did he? Scornfully she grimaced to herself. Well, he would soon learn his mistake!

She came to a crossroads and slowed down to check the signpost, sighing faintly as she realised that it, like so many others she had driven past, had been a victim of the Welsh language lobby.

Luckily, she had had the foresight to buy a map that gave both the Welsh and the English names for the many tiny villages dotted about the Pembroke.

At night, the terrain might seem inhospitable but, as she remembered from short summer weekends she had spent here with Helena, the coastline was one of the most beautiful she had ever seen, with mile upon mile of unspoiled countryside, and narrow, winding roads, between deep banks of hedges that were vaguely reminiscent of Cornwall and Dorset at their very best.

Helena's cottage was rather remote, several miles away from the nearest village, in fact, down a narrow, unmade-up road. She had been left it by a distant relative, and had some claim to Welsh blood. She had spent childhood holidays in the area, and had been able to supply Campion with many interesting facts about it.

The Welsh scornfully referred to Pembroke as being more English than England itself, and certainly a succession of English monarchs had been very generous to friends and foes alike when it came to handing out these once rich Welsh lands.

Sir Philip Sidney, the famous Elizabethan poet and soldier, had been Earl of Pembroke, and there had been others; some sent here as a reward, some as a punishment.

Her imagination suddenly took fire, and she found herself wondering what it would have been like to have been dismissed to this far part of the country, especially for a young girl, more used to the elegance of court living. A girl like Lynsey, for instance.

Within seconds, Campion was totally involved in the plot she was weaving inside her head. She reached automatically for the small tape recorder she always carried with her, the words flowing almost too quickly as she fought to keep pace with her thoughts.

Why was it that she found it so incredibly easy

and exciting to imagine the emotions of her young heroine in this context, but, when it came to making her fall in love and having a sexual relationship, her brain just froze?

Impatient with herself, she pressed harder on the accelerator. Nearly there now, surely. She glanced at the dashboard clock. One in the morning, but she didn't feel tired; at least, not mentally tired. Her brain had gone into overdrive, and she was itching to sit down at her typewriter and work. It would mean altering several chapters she had already done, but that wouldn't be any problem, and it would add an extra dimension to her book.

Angrily, she dismissed the sudden memory she had of Guy telling her that her manuscript lacked a very important dimension. What was she trying to do? Prove to him that she could make the book work without the sexual content he deemed so necessary? And so it would, she told herself mutinously. But, deep down inside herself, she knew it was not just the lack of sexuality to her heroine, but the lack of emotional responsiveness to the men around her that made the book seem so flat. Campion was not a fool, some of the most emotionally and mentally stimulating books ever written—books that caught the imagination and held it fast, books that conveyed a quality of realism and involvement that no one could deny—did so without any reference description of physical lovemaking between the main characters. But what they had, and what her manuscript lacked, was that special, vibrant awareness of the characters' sexuality. A vibrant awareness which she herself had never experienced, other than that one briefly painful episode with Craig.

She was so deeply immersed in her private thoughts that she almost missed the turn-off for the cottage. Braking quickly, she turned into the unmade-up lane.

Surely it had not been as pitted with pot-holes the last time she'd driven down it? Her body lurched against the restraining seat-belt as she tried to avoid the worst of the holes. Muddy water splashed up over her car as she drove straight into one of them, and she cursed mildly.

Although Helena was in Greece, recuperating from a severe bout of pleurisy, her housekeeper had been quite happy to supply Campion with the keys for the cottage. Campion knew Mabel quite well, and the small, dour Scotswoman had warned her that the cottage was not really equipped for winter living.

Campion hadn't been put off, and anyway she wouldn't be staying there very long. She had to be back in London in a month for the book tour, which was a week or so before Christmas, and then she would be spending Christmas with Lucy and Howard. If it was anything like their usual Christmas house-parties, it would be a very sybaritic experience indeed. Howard liked his home comforts—the more luxurious, the better.

The car's headlights picked out the low, rambling shape of the cottage, and thankfully she eased her aching leg off the accelerator.

Now she really was tired. It would be bliss to get into a really hot bath and then just drop into bed, but she suspected the luxury of a bath would have to wait for another day. If she remembered correctly, the house was equipped with an immersion heater, but it would take too long to heat water tonight.

Thank goodness she had had the sense to pack a few basic necessities into one bag. She could take that in with her now, and the rest of the unpacking could wait until the morning.

Carefully easing her aching body out from behind the wheel, Campion found the bag, and a carton of typing paper. Locking the car, she made her way to the cottage.

The lock on the door must have been oiled recently, because the key turned easily in it, and the door yawned open of its own accord, making a creaking sound that made the hair on her scalp prickle, until she remembered that Helena had often laughed about this and other small idiosyncrasies that the cottage possessed.

It was very old, and had once been part of a large local estate, probably a small farmhouse. Helena's great-grandparents had lived here all their married lives, and then Helena had inherited it from a great-aunt when she had died.

The kitchen was stone-flagged and consequently very cold. She shivered as she walked into it, reaching for the light switch and then remembering that it was on the far side of the room. The cottage's wiring was rather haphazard, with light switches and sockets sometimes placed where one would not have expected to find them.

She started to cross the kitchen, and then froze as the lights suddenly snapped on.

For a moment, the brilliance of the unexpected light blinded her; and then shock followed hard on the heels of her initial astonishment.

'What took you so long?' a cool male voice drawled nonchalantly. 'I thought you'd be here hours ago.'

Campion blinked and stared at the man leaning
against the wall; and then she blinked again, trying
to clear her vision.

Guy French, here? Impossible! She must be
imagining things. But no—for one thing, this
morning he had been wearing a suit—a very dark
wool suit with a crisp, white shirt and a neatly
striped tie—and now he was wearing a disreputable
pair of jeans and a very thick jumper over a
checked wool shirt. He was even wearing wellingtons. She goggled slightly as she noticed this. No,
she was most definitely not imagining things! Had
her mind been playing tricks with her, and
superimposed Guy's image against the homely
background of Helena's cottage kitchen, she was
sure it would not have also seen fit to dress him in
anything other than the immaculate suits and shirts
she always saw him wearing.

'Guy.'

Furiously, she realised that he actually had the
audacity to laugh at her. How dared he? And
anyway, what was he doing here?

The grin that curled his mobile mouth brought
her back to reality. Staring stonily at him, she said
as cuttingly as she could, 'I suppose this must be
your idea of a joke, Guy, but quite frankly I don't
think it's funny. I don't understand what you're
doing here, but, since you are here, you'll
understand, I'm sure, when I tell you that I'm
leaving.'

'Not so fast!'

She had never dreamt he could move so quickly,
nor that he could be strong. She gulped as he
barred her way to the door by placing his body in

front of it, and gripping her arms with both his hands.

'Let go of me!' She jerked back from him instinctively, her whole body tensing against his touch, her lips drawn back from her teeth in a feral snarl, her eyes spitting furious green sparks.

He looked at her, and seemed about to say something, and Campion tensed against a further sarcastic retort. But, to her surprise, he complied with her demand, gently pushing her back from him.

'This is no joke,' he told her calmly. 'Far from it. I meant what I said about your manuscript, Campion. It's got to be finished, and you need help to get it finished on time, you know that. Running away down here won't solve anything.'

'I'm not running away.'

How dared he suggest that? She longed to tell him that if it wasn't for his relentless bullying she wouldn't be here at all.

'Then what are you doing here?'

'If you must know, I've come here to work . . .'

'Really? A sudden decision, I take it, since you didn't see fit to inform me of it this morning . . .'

'Perhaps with good reason,' Campion told him nastily, adding bitterly, 'What business of yours is it where I do my work, Guy?'

'Since I'm your agent, for the moment, I should say it was very much my business,' he responded mildly. 'You won't solve anything by running away, you know.'

This was the second time he had made that accusation. Through gritted teeth, Campion told him curtly, 'I am not running away. I've come here to work. Alone . . .' She waved the typing paper at him. 'See . . . I've even done some dictating on the way down here, and if you don't mind, I'd now like to get it typed up . . .'

'Dictating . . . Something along the lines we discussed, I hope . . .'

Campion refused to answer him.

'Ah, I see . . . Just as well I'm here, then, isn't it?'

A tiny sensation of something alien and rather alarming skittered down her spine, and Campion turned to look at him.

'Why *are* you here, Guy?' she asked him slowly. 'And how did you know that I'd decided to come here?'

'Simple—Mabel told me.'

'Mabel?' Campion stared at him.

'Yes. I went round this afternoon to collect Helena's post and go through it for her, and Mabel told me that you'd been round for the cottage keys. Luckily, she had a second set.'

He was dangling them from the tip of one strong, long finger, and a feeling of weakness and disbelief filled Campion as she stared at him.

'And so you decided to come down here yourself . . . but why?'

'Do you remember any of what I said to you this morning?' he asked her softly.

Did she remember? How could she forget?

'Yes.' Her terse answer made him smile slightly, and for one mad moment she had to stop herself from responding to that strange little smile.

'Then you'll remember that I told you I'd given the publishers *my word* that your manuscript would be on their desk on time . . .'

'Yes,' she agreed woodenly, remembering, too,

that she had told him it was impossible. That was when they had had their argument about her having a secretary.

'I even offered you the services of a secretary to help you,' he added gently.

Campion's chest swelled with indignation and fury.

'I don't *want* a secretary!' she told him through bared teeth. 'I don't work that way. I don't need any help with this book, Guy.'

'Oh, yes, you do,' he told her unequivocably. 'But you're right, you don't need a secretary; at least, not the kind I had in mind.'

He was looking at her in a way that made danger signals race from one nerve-ending to another, and a tiny prickle of awareness of him touched her skin. He was standing too close to her, and she instinctively took a step back from him. He smiled when he saw her betraying movement, but there was no humour in his smile.

'Tell me something,' he encouraged softly. 'Your heroines, Campion, do they have much of you in them? Or to put it another way—do you imagine yourself to be them when you're writing?'

A hot wave of colour scalded her skin before she could hold it back.

'No,' she told him forcefully. 'No, I don't. Why do you ask?'

'All in good time.' He looked at his watch. 'It's going on for two, and I, for one, am tired. I think we'll both be in a better frame of mind to discuss things in the morning. I've taken the smaller bedroom. Women always seem to need more room.'

The smaller bedroom? Campion gaped at him.

'You're . . . you're not staying here?'

His eyebrows rose. 'Of course I am! Where else would I be staying?'

'But—you can't.'

'Can't?' He smiled grimly at her.

'All right, so you can stay,' Campion amended, 'but I'm not staying with you.' She headed for the door, determined to walk over him to get it open, if she had to. But she was brought to an abrupt halt as he virtually swung her off her feet, and deposited her down on the floor again with such force that her teeth actually rattled.

'Now, let's get one thing straight,' he told her savagely, all pretence of calm good humour stripped from him now. 'I've given my word, both professionally and personally, that your manuscript will be delivered on time. I've laid myself out on the line for you and your damn book, Campion, and no matter what it takes, you *are* going to deliver . . .'

No matter what it takes . . .'

His eyes seemed to bore into her skull, and she found she was too petrified to even open her mouth. All she could do was to stare at him with mesmerised astonishment.

'It's been one hell of a long day already, needlessly complicated by your unwarranted feminine tantrum and melodramatic flight. All right, so you're having problems with the book, we both know that . . .'

Suddenly, Campion got her senses back. Gathering herself up to her full height, she raised her head and said angrily, 'I'm not staying here listening to any more of this . . .'

'Oh, yes, you are . . . You're staying here until this damn book is finished, and to my satisfaction.

We're both staying here until it's finished,' he
added.

'You . . . you can't make me do that . . .'

'No. No, I can't, but if you walk out of here
now, Campion, that's the end as far as I'm
concerned, and you might as well throw that
manuscript on the fire. Is that what you want? Do
you want to quit? To give up? To admit that you
simply haven't got what it takes to . . .'

She went white, and swayed where she stood, her
whole body filled with pain. His words came so
close to the insults hurled at her by Craig. So very
close that she denied them instinctively, and only
realised as the pain subsided exactly what she had
committed herself to.

She had committed herself to staying here and
finishing her book. And Guy was making it plain
that he had every intention of staying here with
her.

Suddenly, she was too exhausted to argue the
point any further, and besides, her pride would not
allow her to back down now. He had virtually told
her that he didn't think she was capable of bringing
her characters to life, and suddenly it was very,
very important to her that she prove him wrong.
She would finish the book, and when she had done
it it would be so real, so alive, that . . . that . . .
Muzzily, she touched her head. What was hapening
to her? She felt so weak, so drained . . .

'You're tired. Why don't you go to bed? You
can fight with me all you like in the morning.'

Why did the terse words have such an edge of
rough pity? She flinched back from it instinctively,
giving Guy a single baleful glance as she picked up
her bag and headed for the stairs.

'Admit it, Campion, coming here was a form of running away. A cry for help, if you like.'

The quiet words froze her on the stairs. She turned on him like an angry tigress, the cool aura of remoteness she generally projected for once gone.

'If I was running away from anything, it was you,' she told him furiously. 'You and your interference in my life!' She stopped abruptly, conscious of an odd tension in the small room. It made her skin tighten slightly, and she was intensely aware of the man watching her. 'You're the last person I'd cry out to for help, Guy,' she added recklessly. 'The very last.'

'I see. Very well then, you must stay or go as you please, Campion, but remember one thing, if you leave here . . .'

'I'll be admitting that you're right and that I can't finish the book,' she flung at him. 'Oh, I'm not going, Guy. I'm staying, and I'm going to make you take back every insult you've made about my work. You wait and see.'

A strange look crossed his face, a combination of weariness and triumph, and it made her feel as though somehow she had stepped into a cleverly baited trap. But how could that be? Guy wouldn't stay on at the cottage for very long, she assured herself as she made her way to the larger of the two bedrooms. He was a city creature; someone who fed off the bright lights and excitement the city generated; he would be bored out of his mind within a very short space of time, and then he would go and she could get on with her work in peace. Until then, she would just have to ignore him. It shouldn't be that difficult; she had managed well enough for the last ten months. Determinedly, she ignored the small voice that reminded her that during those months she had had Helena to act as a buffer between Guy and herself.

She stalked angrily round the small room, wishing for the hundredth time that her agent had not seen fit to go into partnership with such an irritating man.

She knew that her opinion was a minority one. Everyone else seemed to think that Helena was very fortunate indeed in having as her senior partner a man whose reputation in the literary world meant that he had authors clamouring for him to represent them.

Well, *she* would never clamour for his services, Campion thought fiercely, and a sudden dark tide of colour washed her pale skin as she realised the significance of the *double entendre* conjured up by her thoughts. Guy had no permanent relationship in his life, but that did not mean that he lacked feminine companionship. Far from it! Her mouth tightened as she recalled the seemingly endless line of beautiful women who Helena had told her flocked around him.

Well, they were welcome to him, and she just wished he would take himself off back to them.

It was unfortunate that Mabel had so unwittingly told him what she was planning to do. She ground her teeth as she remembered his accusation that she was running away. From him and his threat of a secretary, yes; from her work, no—never—she loved her work.

She froze as she heard footsteps on the stairs and then a brief rap on her door. Guy opened it before she could protest, poking his head around the small gap.

'Anything you want bringing in from your car? I take it that small carry-all isn't the only luggage you've brought with you? Water's hot, by the way, if you want a bath.'

Did he really think she was incapable of carrying her own suitcase upstairs if she wanted to?

His pseudo-concern made her feel angry. Did he really think she was stupid enough to believe he was the slightest bit concerned about her comfort? All he wanted from her was a successful book. She frowned, confused by the contradictions in her own emotions. She was tired and on edge, and he was the last person with whom she wanted to share such confined quarters as the small, remote cottage, but she had told him she was going to stay, and she wasn't going to be the one to back down.

'If I wanted my case, I'd go and get it,' she told him rudely. 'And I don't want a bath. What I want to do is to go to bed,' she added pointedly.

She saw his eyebrows lift, but there was nothing amused in the way he was looking at her. Rather it was a combination of weariness and pity that darkened his eyes.

Pity. She felt her own eyes grow sore and dry as he stepped back and closed the door. Her throat felt raw and her heart seemed to be beating too fast. How dared he pity her. How dared he . . . She undressed with rapid, almost ungainly movements, checking that he had actually gone back downstairs before she used the bathroom.

A brief wash, her teeth cleaned, and she was back in her bedroom. As she unpinned her hair, she rubbed the tension prickling against her scalp. Her hair was thick and softly curly. She ought to get it cut into a short, manageable style, she thought as she brushed it. The men's pyjamas she had bought especially for the cottage were just as warm as she had hoped, but somehow she couldn't settle. It was all Guy's fault, she decided bitterly, as the adrenalin continued to pump and her body refused to relax into sleep.

If only Helena had not fallen ill . . . or, even better, if only her agent had never agreed to go into partnership with him in the first place . . .

But something made her acknowledge that the faults would still remain with her book, and that they could not be laid at Guy's door. What was she going to do? How was she going to make her heroine come alive? She forced herself to try and think about her, to imagine what her feelings would have been. Was Guy right in saying that, once she knew of the marriage Henry had arranged for her, she would have tried to overset it? Perhaps. It worried her that he seemed to have a better perception of her character's probable behaviour than she had herself.

At last she fell asleep, but her dreams were a confused jumble of images and thoughts. In one, she saw her heroine confronting Henry and telling him that she would not marry the man of his choice; she saw her run through the corridors of his palace while Cardinal Wolsey looked on disapprovingly, and the other courtiers turned diplomatically away. She heard her throw the challenge at Henry that she would get herself with child by the first man who crossed her path, rather than marry the man of his choice. She saw Lynsey run out into the gardens, crying out her cousin's name as she saw him sitting with a group of young men, and then she saw the dark shadow of the man who seemed to come from nowhere to impede her pathway to her cousin, snatching her up at the last

moment, when she would have run into him full
tilt. As he swung her round to put her on her feet,
the sunlight fell across his face, striking a blaze of
colours from the sword hilt at his side. He was
more soberly dressed than the courtiers she was
used to, and she struggled to break free; and then
Campion saw his face.

She screamed a denial, her whole body shaking,
as she came abruptly awake. Her bedroom was in
complete darkness, the silence still and unnerving
after the constant hum of London traffic. She was
cold, and yet she felt breathless, as though she had
been running. The flesh on her arms burned as
though someone had gripped it hard. She looked
down at herself, confused to see the pyjama jacket
where she had expected to see rich satin and
expensive lace, and then a hot flush seared her
skin. In her dream, she had been Lynsey, and the
man who had swept her off her feet had been Guy
French. She shivered as she remembered her impulsive words to King Henry, and then shook her head
in irritation. Her words . . . What was the matter
with her? She had become involved with her
characters before, but never to this extent, surely?

And as for dreaming about Guy French . . .
Well, that was just her mind's way of dealing with
the anger and resentment she felt against him, she
rationalised. That was all.

So why the odd sensation in the pit of her
stomach? Why the shaky, quivering feeling of
unease that tightened her skin and made her feel
acutely vulnerable? These were feelings that an
impressionable teenager might experience, but
hardly applicable to a grown woman of twenty-six.
And besides . . . besides, she was not in the least

attracted to Guy—far from it.

Attracted to him? She froze, staring into the darkness, her body tense and still. Where had that thought come from? She shuddered slightly, trying to hold at bay the sick, nervy feeling invading her senses.

She must be sickening for something, she told herself; these odd feelings she kept having, this feeling of vulnerability, they were so unlike anything she was used to feeling. It was because she was upset about her book. Yes, that was the answer; she was upset about her book, and Guy French was exacerbating the situation. If only he had not decided to come down here, she wished cravenly. She didn't want him here. He unnerved and unsettled her. She wanted him to go away and leave her in peace, and most of all she wanted him to stop looking at her with that infuriating blend of sadness and compassion.

CHAPTER THREE

INEVITABLY, perhaps, after her disturbed night, Campion overslept. When she eventually woke up, it was to the sound of heavy rain outside, whipped against the windows by a buffeting wind.

Her bedroom was gloriously warm, and she wriggled her toes blissfully, the comfort of the room and its contrast to the weather outside taking her back to her childhood. She snuggled deeper into the bed and closed her eyes.

'I thought you came here to work.'

The drawling male voice destroyed her pleasure, and made her sit up in bed with a frown.

Guy was standing beside the bed, holding a tray. The delicious aroma of freshly made coffee tantalised her senses. There was toast as well, crisply golden and melting with butter.

'I hope you've brought some sensible clothes with you,' Guy remarked as he settled the tray on the small chest beside the bed. 'Helena isn't exactly geared up for anything other than brief summer living here.'

'How can you say that?' Campion demanded. 'The house is centrally heated. It's beautifully warm in here. If you're finding it uncomfortable in any way, perhaps you ought to go back to London.'

He gave her a wry look.

'No way. And for your information, the cottage is centrally heated only because I drove down to the village this morning and begged and borrowed a couple of bags of boiler fuel. Luckily, I've managed to get a supplier to deliver some more this afternoon.' He grimaced in disgust. 'Trust a woman to have a solid fuel heating system installed, and then forget to order any fuel for it.'

Campion bit her lip and glanced involuntarily at the window. Outside, rain pelted against the glass. If Guy hadn't been here, she would have woken up to a cold, damp atmosphere, and somehow she doubted that she would have had the self-confidence to march down to the village and acquire the necessary fuel. Even so, she couldn't bring herself to say anything, other than a grudging, 'No one asked you to come here.'

There was a long, unnerving silence, during which Guy looked steadily at her, before saying in a quietly even voice, 'Didn't they? I rather thought I'd heard a cry for help.'

Colour stung her face as Campion glared at him. He had said nearly the same thing last night, and if he thought for one moment that she had actually expected him to follow her down here . . .

'Not from me, you didn't,' she told him angrily. 'If you must know, I came here to get *away* from you . . .'

'Really?' How dangerous his voice sounded when it took on that silky quality! Dangerous was not a word she would ever have applied to Guy before; in fact, she had rather disparagingly considered him to be something of a lightweight. But somehow, down here, alone with him, seeing him dressed in rugged jeans and casual shirts, she was beginning to view him in a different light. He should have looked odd out of his immaculate suits and shirts, but he didn't. In fact, he looked very much at home in them.

'Odd. I distinctly remember you telling me you came here to work . . .'

'To work, and to get away from your interference with that work,' Campion countered aggressively after a minute pause. 'And if you wouldn't mind, I would like to get up and get on with that work.'

The dark eyebrows rose, and she could have sworn there was almost something vaguely reminiscent of a courtly but mocking bow in the way he moved his arm.

'Be my guest,' he offered, picking a piece of toast off the plate, and leaning back against the wall, ignoring her.

There was just no way she was going to get out of bed with him standing there, eating her toast, Campion decided grimly.

She had no doubt that he was simply amusing himself at her expense, pretending not to know how much she detested being forced into such intimacy with him.

She moved angrily, her hair swirling into tousled curls. Out of the corner of her eye, she saw Guy tense, and then, to her surprise, he said abruptly, 'I'd better go and check on the boiler.'

He'd gone without even finishing his toast, she realised a few seconds later, as she stared at the door he had closed after him.

An odd feeling crept over her, a sense of loss, combined with a far more familiar feeling of acute self-disgust. Under the bedclothes, her body started to shake and she closed her eyes tightly, trying to ward off her own thoughts.

She knew quite well what had brought that look to Guy's eyes, why he had been so anxious to get out of the room. He had looked at her and had been repulsed by her, just as Craig had been, as every man who looked at her must be, she admitted bleakly.

What was the point in letting herself be hurt by it? Surely, by now, she was used to the truth? Surely she had taught herself to accept that men found her undesirable, that it was revulsion rather than arousal they experienced when they looked at her?

Craig had made it clear enough all those years ago. The only way he had been able to make love to her, he had said, had been by closing his eyes and pretending she was someone else, and even then . . . Even then it had only been the thought of her parents' wealth that had enabled him to go through with it.

Even now, those words still had the power to wound her, to scour her soul and destroy her self-confidence. It was no use telling herself she was a successful writer, that she had a good and fulfilling life, that many, many people would envy her; all she had to do was to remember Craig's words, to recall how Guy had just looked at her, and she was that same sick, shaking teenager whose eyes had been so cruelly opened to exactly how unattractive she actually was.

Was it any wonder she couldn't give her heroine the confidence to go out and choose her own lover, that she couldn't flesh out the sensual, physical side of Lynsey's nature? There, she had admitted it. She swallowed hard. She had admitted that Guy was right, and that she couldn't finish the book.

Panic filled her as she fought to deny her own thoughts. It wasn't true. She *would* finish it . . . There must be another way, and she would find it.

Suddenly she remembered her dream. In her dream, she had felt Lynsey's emotions: her anger, her desperation, her resentment towards the man who had stopped her from going to her cousin. If she could just hold on to those memories . . . If she could just get them down on paper . . . Suddenly her doubts were subdued, her mind busy trying to work out how best she could use the avenue opened up to her by her dream.

She washed and dressed hurriedly, pulling out of her bag her clean underwear, and then frowning. No clean bra . . . She must have left it in her flat on the bed, and the rest of her underwear was in the case in the boot of her car. She eyed the one she had been wearing the previous day with distaste.

On the bed were the jeans, sweater and shirt she was planning to wear. The shirt was fine wool, and the sweater a warm, bulky one. If Guy hadn't been here, she wouldn't even have hesitated about not wearing a bra. What difference did his being here make? Surely she wasn't afraid that the sight of her braless but thickly covered body was going to send him into a fury of lust?

No, of course she wasn't, but what if he should notice and think that perhaps she . . . She licked her top lip nervously. She had learned to be so careful about not conveying the wrong impression, about not allowing men to think that she was at all interested in them. She didn't want the humiliation of being rejected a second time, and so she had learned that it was best to cultivate an appearance that made it plain that she didn't consider herself to be a sexual woman.

She was wasting time when she ought to be working, she reminded herself. Guy was hardly likely to notice that she wasn't wearing one, not particularly important article of underwear, and even if he did . . . Even if he did, the thought of a woman like her daring to imagine she might physically attract him was so ludicrous that it would never even cross his mind.

Having reassured herself, she dressed quickly, and then pinned up her hair.

The scent of frying bacon greeted her as she walked into the kitchen. Guy was standing in front of the cooker, deftly manoeuvring an array of pans.

He must have sharp ears, she acknowledged as he turned and smiled at her.

'Just in time. How do you like your eggs?'

'I don't,' Campion told him shortly.

His eyebrows rose in the way that was becoming very familiar.

'Nonsense! You need a decent breakfast inside you if you're going to work.' His eyes narrowed slightly, and she realised he was looking at her hair. She itched to raise her hand to ensure that it was all tidily tucked away, and had to fight not to make the betraying gesture.

'What happened to the curls?' he asked softly, looking at her in such a way that she could feel her skin start to burn.

Ignoring him, she turned towards the door that led into the cottage's sitting-room. Off it was the small study that had once been an outhouse, and which Helena had had converted into a very efficient work-room for those of her writers who took advantage of her standing offer to use the cottage as a bolt hole.

'Where are you going?'

'To work. That's what I came up here for—remember?' she asked dangerously.

'Not before you've had something to eat.'

Campion found that she was literally grinding her

teeth.

It was all too tempting to make some childish riposte such as 'Make me,' but she had the uncomfortable feeling that he would take the greatest delight in doing exactly that, and so, instead, she walked across the floor and sat down reluctantly at the table.

'That's better. Even brain cells need feeding . . . and stimulating,' he added softly.

Campion stared at him, her breath suddenly trapped deep in her lungs. A most curious sensation invaded her, a feeling of weakness edged with excitement. And then she tore her gaze away, and the feeling subsided.

'For someone who didn't want any breakfast, you've managed to demolish a surprising amount of food.'

She should have expected a taunt like that, Campion told herself bitterly as she drank the last of her coffee. To her own surprise, she *had* been hungry. It was a luxury to have her breakfast prepared for her—to have any meal prepared for her, come to think of it.

'I have a perfectly normal appetite,' she told him frigidly. 'Unlike the women you date, I'm not obsessed by my weight,' she added scathingly.

It was a shot in the dark, but she suspected from all that she had been told that the glamorous women he normally dated were hardly the types to sit down to a full cooked breakfast. A vitamin cocktail and a glass of Perrier was probably their style.

'No, you're not obsessed by your *weight*,' Guy agreed steadily, but the look in his eyes made her feel acutely uncomfortable. She felt as though he had looked right into her mind and seen things there that she would much rather he had not seen.

She offered to do the washing up, as much to escape from his too-close scrutiny as anything else. He had discarded the sweater he'd had on earlier, and she could see the fine, dark hairs curling in the open neckline of his shirt. She swallowed nervously, wondering why she was reacting so stupidly.

'I'll wash up. You'll want to bring in the rest of your things.' For some reason, his remark annoyed her.

'Oh, I'll do that later,' she told him carelessly. 'Right now, I want to start work.' She turned her back on him and opened the door.

The small study had a radiator and was blissfully warm. She was just about to close the door and get to work when Guy suddenly appeared in the doorway, and casually reached down to unplug the machine.

Campion stared at him, her eyes revealing her baffled anger.

'What on earth are you doing? I want to start work.'

'Not yet,' he told her calmly. 'First, we have to analyse properly where you're going wrong.'

For a moment, she was lost for words. She took a deep breath, holding on to her anger with difficulty, and said through clenched teeth, 'I thought you'd already done that.'

'Yes, I have, but you don't seem to agree. So, before you so much as put another word on paper, I think we should both be clear on exactly what alterations are required.'

We? It was *her* book, her work, her characters. Campion felt ready to explode, so great was the resentment building up inside her, but she had taught herself long ago to control her feelings and to keep them hidden from others, and so all she could do was to glare at him and curl her fingers tightly into her palms.

'Like a cup of coffee before we start?'

'No, thanks, I think I've already got enough adrenalin pumping round my veins right now,' Campion told him freezingly.

'Well, if you'll bear with me for a second, I'll make myself one, and then we can settle down to work.'

Did nothing ever faze him? Campion wondered bitterly, watching him walk away. Was that smooth, laconic manner never ruffled by irritation or anger? He projected an image of being totally in control of his life, and now he was trying to take control of hers, and she didn't like it.

She was still fuming when he came back, carrying a steaming mug of coffee.

'I thought you said it was a secretary I needed, not someone to stand over me and monitor every single word I write,' she demanded, glowering at him.

The study was only small, and she hated the sensation of having him so close to her. The desk was pushed into a corner, and she had a wall to one side of her and Guy to the other. She could smell the scent of his skin, tangy with the soap he had used to wash. His hair still held the fresh coldness of the outdoors and looked slightly damp.

'My suggestion that you take on a secretary was simply made to relieve you of the pressure of trying to finish the book on time. I must admit that then I envisaged that you would submit your rewrites to me in the normal way; when I learned from Mabel that you'd decided to disappear, I realised that slightly more drastic measures were called for.'

'I did not decide to disappear,' Campion contradicted acidly. 'I've already told you I came here to work, and I can do that work far better without you hanging over my shoulder. I'd get the alterations finished much faster if you would leave me alone and go back to London.'

'Would you?' His eyebrows lifted. 'Let's see, shall we?' He opened a briefcase he had put down beside the desk, and extracted a copy of her manuscript.

'Right . . . Chapter four, when Lynsey first realises that her feelings for her cousin have become those of a woman and not those of a child. You say she loves him, but there is no real sense of any awareness from the reader's point of view of her own sexuality. If you like, she's like a robot reading the words off an autocue. So, what do you plan to do to make the reader aware of Lynsey's burgeoning womanhood?'

Campion felt her skin start to burn with a mixture of rage and confusion. Panic hit her. She tried desperately to blot out Guy and the emotions that were filling the small room, clogging her thought processes, and instead imagine that she was her heroine: a headstrong, spoilt girl of sixteen, who was just beginning to realise the power of her femininity, but somehow, no matter how much she tried to concentrate, no sense of any awareness of being in touch with Lynsey's feelings would come. She might have been trying to imagine the feelings of an alien being from another planet!

Frantically, she tried to think back, to remember how she had felt at that age, but she had been shy and different. Frustratedly, she realised that she had created as her heroine the kind of girl/woman she had once ached to be, and that, for once, not even her powerful imagination was strong enough to give her an insight into how that girl might have felt.

'Come on, Campion. The girl's in love, as much with the idea of being in love as with anything else. She's seen how her cousin reacts to her. What would she do?'

'Why should she *do* anything?' Campion countered huskily. 'She's only sixteen . . . She would wait for Francis to approach her.'

'No, she's not that kind; he's the weaker of the two, you say so yourself later in the book. Think, Campion, she's been indulged all her life; she's self-confident, fearless, and most of all curious . . . I suggest that she would try to engineer a meeting between herself and Francis where they could be alone and she could test her new-found power.'

'No!' The sharp revulsion in her own voice startled her, and Campion avoided looking at Guy.

'No? Why not?' he asked her quietly.

— She felt like a butterfly pinned down for inspection. She desperately wanted to escape, to be left alone. She hated this merciless probing, this constant pushing at her to produce something that . . . That she was incapable of producing? Despair stabbed through her. She couldn't tell him that. She had her pride, after all. There must be a way . . . While she was still trying to sort out her confused thoughts, she heard Guy saying softly, 'Campion, I've read all your books over the last few weeks. There's an odd lack of sexuality in all of them, do you know that?'

Odd? Her body stiffened, sensing danger, her head lifting defiantly as she met the look in his eyes and forced herself not to cringe beneath it.

'Why should I be considered odd just because I

don't spatter my work with lurid passages of pseudo-pornography?'

His eyebrows rose. 'Is that how you see sex? As pornographic? You surprise me. The written word *can* be pornographic, I agree, but it can also be very, very sensual.'

'It isn't my job to write that kind of thing,' she protested sharply.

'No, but it *is* your job to flesh out the character of a young woman whom you seem to be dooming to a course of behaviour that's totally out of keeping with the personality you've given her, and thus making her totally unbelievable in the mind of the reader.'

'I could change her character.'

As she looked at him, Champion was unaware of the desperation in her voice and eyes. All she saw was a sudden and totally unexpected softening in the grey eyes that held her gaze. Guy lifted his hand from her manuscript, and instinctively she flinched back. Immediately, that slight softening was gone, and tiny sparks seemed to ignite in the depths of his eyes, as though he was very, very angry indeed. But he still continued to smile, and she decided that she must have been wrong. When men got angry they lost control, said and did things that were hurtful in the extreme, as she knew to her cost.

'Tell me, Campion, why do you find it so hard to give your characters any sexuality? Your men, for instance. I've noticed that, even when you're sticking to historical fact, you manage to avoid the human side of their natures completely. Why?'

She was frightened now. He was probing too close to things that hurt. Things that she had always thought were her secrets, and hers alone. Helena had never talked to her like this. All right, so sometimes she had laughed and teased her, sometimes she had made gentle suggestions which necessitated some small alterations in her work, but she had never, ever done anything like this.

Suddenly, her anger left her, and in its place came an icy thrust of fear. Why was Guy doing this to her? What was he trying to get her to admit? That she was inadequate as a woman? Her skin crawled as she realised how much she might have unwittingly betrayed about herself in her writing. Was this why she had so fiercely resisted the idea of having a secretary? Had she known, without actually acknowledging it, that she was vulnerable? Had she been afraid of what someone working closely with her might discover about her?

Panic built up inside her, coiling and burning, seeking some means of escape.

Guy was sitting far too close to her. She felt trapped, hemmed in. She stared desperately at the wall, as though she could somehow conjure up a gap in it through which she could escape, but there was none. She turned to face him, her eyes darkening as she saw the calm, waiting quality in his composed silence.

'What is this? The Inquisition?'

To her relief, he didn't laugh at her. Instead, he asked seriously, 'Is that how you see me, Campion? As an inquisitor; a man capable of great cruelty; a man who enjoys inflicting pain on others; a man so zealous in his pursuit of what he believes in that he's prepared to go to any lengths to secure those beliefs?'

Of course she didn't. It had been stupid of her to choose that particular smile.

'I'm just trying to help you, that's all.'

'I don't need your help . . .'

'I think you do,' retorted Guy quietly. 'Shall I tell you what I see when I look at you, Campion?'

Now, when she wasn't prepared for it, he did reach out and touch her, his hand cupping the side of her face firmly. Her skin hurt, and she shook with shock and fear. She could feel the hard pads of his fingertips against her skin. She was shaking like someone in the grip of an intense fever, and there was nothing she could do about it—not a single thing.

She could see the irises of his eyes—clear, cool grey. His eyes were thickly and darkly lashed, his jaw dark where he shaved.

Campion opened her mouth to cry out to him to let her go, but no sound emerged. Panic flooded her. She wanted to cry and scream. She wanted to tear his hand from her skin. She wanted . . . she wanted to turn and run, and go on running until she could find somewhere to hide, both from him and from herself.

What was he doing this for?

'Your skin feels like silk velvet.' He smiled at her, and tiny lines fanned out from around his eyes.

Campion felt as though she were disintegrating, as though she was being torn apart by the pain of what was happening. How could he do this to her? Did he think she was blind, that she didn't, couldn't see for herself the differences between them? Did he honestly imagine she was stupid enough to believe that he could actually find anything physically attractive about her?

'Stop it! Stop it! Don't touch me!'

At last she had found her voice, even if the words did come out high and strained. She jerked back, her eyes wild with emotions that made Guy release her immediately.

'You don't have to waste your time complimenting

me, Guy,' she told him harshly. 'I know exactly what
kind of woman I am.'

'Do you?' Unexpectedly, his own voice was far
from its normal, even tone. 'I wonder.'

She couldn't stand it any longer; the atmosphere in
the small room was far too fraught and tense for her
to even think about working.

She got up clumsily, almost flattening herself
against the wall in her desire to avoid touching him.

'I'm going out for a walk.'

'You'll get soaked.'

'I don't care.'

If he suggested going with her, she would probably
push him down the first hillside they came to. She
had to get away from him. To her relief, he stepped
easily to one side to allow her to leave.

Her outdoor coat and her wellingtons were still in
the car. She found them and pulled them on,
ignoring the rain pelting down on her.

Out here she could breathe, she could relax, and
most of all she could forget how she had felt when
Guy French touched her.

Campion had walked in Pembroke before on visits
with Helena. For mile upon glorious mile, the
headland and cliffs belonged to the National Trust,
and their paths were open to walkers, but that had
been in summer, and she had gone less than a mile
when she realised how very cold and wet it actually
was.

The cottage and the village were only a couple of
miles from the coast, but she would be a fool to try
and walk there today, Campion acknowledged. The
wind seemed to have trebled in force since she had
come out, and already she was almost bent double

under the force of it. It had whipped back her hood and tormented strands of her hair free from her French pleat to plaster them wetly across her skin. Her hands were icy cold, and she discovered that her wellingtons seemed to leak. Even so, despite all her discomfort, she preferred to be here outside rather than cooped up in the cottage with Guy.

What had he been trying to do? Surely he must know how aware she was that a man like him would never find her attractive? So why touch her . . . why make that stupid remark about her skin? She shivered, and not because of the cold or the damp penetrating her coat.

The sensation she had experienced when he touched her skin had been so electrifying, so shocking, that she was still shaken by the memory of it.

Her whole body had seemed to leap to meet his touch, and for one horrendous moment she had actually wondered what it would be like to experience his hand against her naked skin.

She had never known anything like it before. Not even with Craig. It was all Guy's fault; all his probing and digging had unleashed an awareness in her of all that was missing from her life. For one incredible moment in the study, she had actually found herself envying and resenting her own heroine, jealously wishing that she was Lynsey, free to explore and enjoy her sensuality.

She must be going crazy, she told herself. It was this damn book. She should never have agreed to take it on. But she *had* agreed, and her pride would not let her give up now. She had to finish it . . .

Suddenly, she was overwhelmed by a frantic need to get back to work. She turned blindly and started to almost run back. The sooner the alterations were done, the sooner she would be free to escape from Guy. She would even let him tell her what to write, if that got the work done faster . . .

A sudden gust of wind caught her, winding her with its force. She staggered and slipped on the treacherously muddy path, landing uncomfortably, but not too painfully, on the wet ground.

When she got up, she saw with despair that her coat was covered in mud and soaking wet. She shivered. The wind had developed an icy edge that cut through her jeans and top.

By the time she got back to the cottage, her teeth were chattering and her hands turning blue.

Guy was in the kitchen when she staggered in, stirring something in a pan. The rich smell of hot soup filled the room, and Campion couldn't help despairingly contrasting the calm efficiency of this man, who seemed to have a deftly sure touch in all he did, with her own apparently doomed attempts to show him that she was entirely self-sufficient.

She couldn't even go out for a short walk without inviting disaster, she reflected bitterly as she struggled to tug off her wellingtons.

'Here, let me . . .'

Of course, the damn things would have to slide off easily the moment he touched them.

She stiffened as she looked down at his dark head as he kneeled to help her. Why was it that there was something almost vulnerable about the sight of the nape of his neck? His skin was faintly brown, his muscles moving easily as he helped her out of her boots.

She felt oddly lethargic; unable to move. She felt the warmth of his hand on her skin, and the ripples of heat that spread out from the place where he touched her.

'Are you all right?'

Humiliation filled her, and she struggled to step back from him. How had he known about that peculiar sensation of pleasure she had just experienced? And then she realised he was looking at her muddy coat.

'I fell over, that's all,' she told him shortly. 'The path was muddy.'

'Why don't you go up and have a shower, and then we can have lunch?'

The thought of warm water on her cold, wet skin was too blissful to be ignored.

It took far longer than she had anticipated to remove her wet jeans. They clung stubbornly to her legs, resisting all her attempts to tug them off, but at last she managed to remove them. Underneath, her skin was red and chafed from the irritation of the harsh cloth.

She had to take down her hair as well, but only realised when she was in the bathroom that she had forgotten her shower cap, so she had to use some of Guy's shampoo, and waste even more time.

When she stepped out of the shower, she discovered she had left her fresh underwear on the bed. What was happening to her? She was normally so organised.

Still wrapped in the damp towel, her hair curling wetly on to her shoulders, she stepped irritably out of the bathroom and walked straight into Guy.

His hands steadied her, holding on to the bare skin of her upper arms.

'Are you OK?'

'Of course I am.'

'You've been up here so long, I thought your fall must have been more serious than you were letting on.'

She was carrying her wet briefs and top in one hand, and her toilet bag in the other. It wasn't very warm on the landing, and already she was starting to shiver.

'I've already told you I'm perfectly all right, and if you don't mind I'd like to go and get dressed.'

When Guy didn't release her immediately, she pulled away from him, and then gave a sharp cry of dismay as she felt her towel starting to slide away from her body.

She dropped everything she was carrying immediately, but even so Guy moved faster, catching the towel just as it slithered down to reveal the full curves of her breasts.

'Whoops . . .'

Deftly, he caught up the ends and secured them more firmly above her breasts, and she, for some reason, simply stood there and let him.

She was having difficulty in breathing, and her brain seemed to have stopped functioning at precisely that second when she had felt the brief touch of Guy's fingers against the swell of her breasts as he reached for the towel. Her body turned and then froze, her mind blank of everything bar the feeling his touch had engendered.

Sickly, she acknowledged the truth. When Guy had touched her, she had actually been physically aroused.

Oh, God, what was happening to her? She must be sick, deranged in some way. She had to be to feel like that. How could she be stupid enough to desire a man whom she knew could never, ever want her?

Dimly, she was aware of Guy bending to pick up the things she had dropped, and gently handing them to her. She focused on him, her eyes unknowingly dark with pain and shock.

He touched her arm and she flinched.

'Are you sure you're all right?'

All right? How could she be all right, when she felt like this, when her whole body was still tormented with the most acute thrust of need she had ever felt?

The sound of his voice brought her back to reality. She *couldn't* let him see what was happening to her. She had to fight against whatever madness it was that possessed her; she *had* to stop herself feeling like this. If only he could go away and leave her in peace . . . but she couldn't run away. Not a second time . . .

The betraying words hung in her mind, as though they were written there in the fire. A second time . . . Her mouth went dry, and she forced herself to swallow to relieve some of the tension invading her throat.

Was that why she had come here, then? Because of Guy French? Because she had known subconsciously that she was physically attracted to him?

They were questions she couldn't bear to answer. There was only one way she could escape from her torment, she acknowledged, only one way she could stop herself from going mad thinking about her folly, and that was to lose herself in her work.

'I don't want any lunch,' she told him harshly, 'I want to get back to work. I . . . I had an idea while I was out . . .'

It wasn't true, but she *had* had an idea the previous night, and she could work on that. Anything to get away from him.

CHAPTER FOUR

CAMPION dressed quickly in the first things that came to hand; a thin jumper and an old pleated skirt. She didn't want to waste time doing her hair. She went downstairs with it still hanging in damp tendrils around her face.

Her breasts felt slightly sore and tender, an unfamiliar sensation that was extremely disturbing.

She saw Guy look at her as she went downstairs, but he made no attempt to stop her going straight into the study.

In the sitting-room there was a mirror over the fireplace, and Campion flushed with mortification as she caught sight of her reflection there, and saw the way her nipples thrust against the combined covering of her bra and sweater.

Work, that was the answer, she thought feverishly, dragging her gaze away and hurrying into the study. What was it Guy had said to her this morning about Lynsey wanting to experiment with the power of her womanhood?

She found the pages they had discussed, and read them quickly. Her description of Lynsey's burgeoning feeling for her cousin was flat and uninteresting. She closed her eyes, leaning back in her chair. She saw Lynsey studying herself in the mirror in her room, admiring the curves of her flesh, perhaps touching the high, firm outline of her breasts, and wondering what it would be like if Francis . . . King Henry's court had been a licentious one; a girl growing up there could not remain unaware of the reality of sexual communion.

Campion shivered; her body felt so tightly coiled that the tension made her ache. What had seemed impossible to describe now seemed easy; the words flowed from her, so quickly, she could barely capture them. She typed until her wrists ached, and then stared in surprise at the number of pages she had done.

Almost as though he had been waiting for the typewriter to stop clattering, Guy walked in. He reached out to pick up the pages, but she stopped him.

'No! I haven't read them myself yet,' she told him, conscious of how strained and fierce her denial had been.

She didn't want him reading what she had written until she had read it herself, until she had made sure there was nothing in it to betray her . . .

But why should there be? Why should that momentary and totally ridiculous surge of desire she had experienced at Guy's touch have any bearing on what she had just written? It was impossible.

'What were you doing? Standing outside the door, waiting for me to finish?' she demanded, desperately trying to find a way to get back to normal.

'No. You just happened to stop as I came in to ask what you fancied having for dinner. We can eat out, if you like.'

'No. At least . . . Look, why don't you go out. I'll fix myself something later. I'm not hungry at the moment.'

'Still trying to get rid of me?'

Her face flamed, and one of the pages she was reaching for slid out of her reach.

Guy retrieved it for her.

'Small, firm breasts, mmm . . . I'm glad you liken them to unripened apples, because personally I much prefer a woman's body when it's fully developed and mature.'

Just briefly, his glance slid downwards, and Campion felt as though she would choke from shock and disbelief as it lingered briefly on the telltale curves of her own breasts.

Like a current of electricity, she felt her physical response to his glance. She turned away abruptly, not daring to look at him.

'Lynsey is sixteen,' she reminded him acidly, 'and therefore hardly likely to be mature.'

Without looking at him, she knew that he was smiling.

'She's very real to you, isn't she? You know, that's one thing that never fails to fascinate me about writers—good writers, that is. They become so passionately involved with their characters; they put so much of themselves into them, I suppose. How much of you is in Lynsey, Campion?'

How deftly he had slipped that question beneath her guard!

'Very little,' she told him icily. 'How could there be anything of me in Lynsey? As you yourself pointed out, she is a beautiful, self-confident woman.'

'Are you trying to tell me you consider yourself to be lacking in self-confidence, Campion?'

She couldn't believe the cruelty of the softly spoken words. How dared he make fun of her like this? How dared he speak to her in that soft, almost teasing voice, implying . . . implying what?

'I'm tired, Guy.'

'You need some food inside you. You'll soon feel better. There's some soup left.'

Why on earth couldn't he see that she wanted him to leave her alone?

She moved her head, and felt the unaccustomed softness of her hair against her face.

'It suits you like that.'

Campion froze immediately. How dared he torment her like this, pretending that he actually found her physically attractive, when they both knew that no man, never mind one like him, could possible do that?

'I . . .' The words of denial stuck in her throat. Her chest felt tight and sore. She saw Guy reach out towards her, and flinched back from any physical contact with him.

'What's wrong?' Every time I compliment you, you react as though I'd insulted you.'

It was the pain inside her that made her cry out sharply, 'What am I supposed to do? Fall at your feet in gratitude?'

She tried to push past him, and cried out as he caught hold of her wrists, dragging her towards him.

Was it only this morning that she had envied his laconic self-control? Well, it had gone now. Grey sparks flamed in the depths of his eyes, and she could see the rapid rise and fall of his chest as he breathed harshly. 'Nothing so dramatic, just a smile would be sufficient. The reaction any——'

'Any normal woman would make?' Campion finished for him. 'Is that what you were going to say?'

— She had stopped trying to pull away from him. He obviously had no intention of letting her go, and every time she moved his grip hurt her wrists.

'No, as a matter of fact, it wasn't. What is it about you, Campion? Why do you go to such lengths to deny your sexuality? I've been watching you, and shall I tell you what I see?'

— He didn't need to, Campion already knew. If the image in her mirror every morning wasn't enough, she still had Craig's insults burned into her soul to remind her.

'I see a woman who for some reason is so desperate to conceal her sexuality that she doesn't even realise what she's betraying by going to such extremes. By your very desire to appear sexual, you make yourself stand out, do you know that?'

'That's not true!'

'Yes, it is.'

He looked at her broodingly, and the pressure of his grip eased. His thumbs started stroking lightly against the delicate inside of her wrists. Her pulse stopped, and then thudded hectically. She felt as though her blood was draining from every part of her body, to throb frantically beneath his touch.

'You're such a very beautiful woman, and yet you behave . . .'

'Stop it! Stop it . . .'

Somehow she managed to wrench herself from his grip, her senses in agonised turmoil as she raced past him and upstairs to her room.

How could he do this to her? What was the point? A very beautiful woman! Did he think she was *blind*? Her throat was tight with tears of anger she refused to shed. She waited tensely, expecting him to come bursting into her room with every breath she took, but the seconds and then the minutes went past in silence. Then, shockingly, she heard the slam of the kitchen door.

She ran to the window and watched as Guy climbed into his car.

He was leaving. Thank God for that!

And yet she had no sense of relief, no lessening of the tension coiling inside her. Instead she felt empty, aching, unsettled.

She went back downstairs, but she couldn't work. Dusk gave way to Stygian dark. She made herself a cup of coffee and wandered round the kitchen. How empty the cottage seemed without him, and yet she had wanted him to go. Hadn't she?

Just for a moment, she tried to imagine what might have happened if he had stayed, if she had really been beautiful as he had cruelly called her ...

Her body quivered, tiny flames heating her skin. Her hand shook and she put her coffee down, hugging her arms tightly around herself, as though to reject the sensations she was experiencing.

How long had she felt like this and not known it? How long had she ached like this and not known why? She was behaving like an adolescent, or the archetypal frustrated spinster, she taunted herself.

Guy French had no interest in her other than as a writer. She had no idea why he was pretending to find her attractive; no idea at all. Somehow, she would have thought he was far too fastidious to lower himself to such contemptible behaviour.

She couldn't eat, she couldn't work. She might as well to to bed and try to catch up on last night's missed sleep.

It only occurred to her once she was in bed that, with Guy gone, there was nothing to stop her returning to London herself, but, with Guy gone, what was the point? The book still had to be finished, and she was more determined than ever now to prove that she could finish it.

She slept for two hours, and then woke up abruptly, feeling cold and hungry.

There was no point in dressing again, so she went downstairs as she was in her pyjamas. The kitchen felt cold, and it was only when she walked into it that she realised she had forgotten to stoke the boiler. Luckily, it was still alight, but by the time she had finished feeding it and coaxing it back to life she was filthy.

Since coming to the cottage she seemed to have wasted more energy getting clean than at any other time in her life!

This time she had a bath and not a shower, luxuriating in the heat of the water against her chilly skin. She was just about to step out when the lights flickered and then went out.

For a moment, she was too surprised to move. In London, the lights never went out. She got out of the bath and groped her way toward the towel rail, stubbing her toe against something hard and uncomfortable on the way.

Outside she could hear the fierce sound of the wind. It sounded much louder than it had done earlier. Strong enough to damage the power lines?

There was always the generator in the outhouse, but she hadn't the faintest idea how to get it going. She had brought a torch with her, but it was still in the car. She had also brought some candles. Had Guy brought them in when he had brought in the other things? If so, where had he put them?

Of course, he would go and leave her on her own to face this . . .

She only realised the incongruity of her thoughts as she headed downstairs clad only in a pair of briefs, her pyjama top and a pair of pale pink socks—all she had been able to find in the darkness of the bathroom.

She had to feel her way downstairs, almost missing two of the stairs, and bumping her head on the lintel at the bottom. To her relief, she saw that the kitchen was vaguely illuminated by the glow of the boiler. Thank goodness she had woken up in time to attend to it before the power failure!

The kitchen had very few cupboards, and none of them yielded the requisite candles, which meant that she would have to go outside and get the torch from her car.

Where were her wellingtons? She remembered how they had leaked, and flinched from the thought of putting them on, but her shoes were upstairs, and there was no guarantee that she would find them in the darkness.

It would have to be the wellingtons.

She opened the back door and cried out in shock as something whipped cruelly against her face, striking her with scratching fingers.

Her mind and body were thrown into immediate panic. No modern city dweller lived in ignorance of the violence on the streets, and Campion reacted instinctively, tearing at the clawing fingers on her face, only to realise that her assailant was nothing more than a springy branch torn down from somewhere by the wind!

Even so, it took several minutes for her heart to

resume its normal steady beat, and then, very slowly, her eyes accustomed themselves to the darkness, and she realised that there was a very thin light from the cloud-covered moon, and she could just about make out the shape of the buildings and her car.

It was bitterly cold though, and the temperature must surely have dropped. As she stepped out of the shelter of the house, icy pellets of rain stung her face. No, not rain, she realised, but hail. She reached her car and tugged on the door. Nothing happened.

Frustrated, she stared at it and then realised that Guy must have locked it when he removed her things. Trust a man to do something like that. Where were her keys? She could have cried with misery. What chance did she have of finding them in that dark house?

There was nothing else for it, she would have to go back and wait for the electricity to come back on.

As she stumbled through the doorway, she reflected how galling and infuriating it was to be held at the mercy of the elements in this way, and then she found herself thinking that Lynsey must have felt the same way at being at the mercy of the King. Guy was right—she would have rebelled, would have tried to take charge of her own life. By trying to persuade her cousin to seduce her?

Out of nowhere came a mental image of her dream: the tall man who had stepped across Lynsey's path. A tiny flutter of excitement started up inside her. Guy had brought her portable machine in, and it was in the study; if she could find it, she could bring it into the kitchen.

Suddenly, she was itching to work. She didn't need light to type, and she certainly didn't need electricity to think.

Half an hour later, she was hard at work, the power cut forgotten.

She had stripped off her wet socks, and her long, bare legs were resting on the bar of the table. The boiler kept the kitchen pleasantly warm, and she ceased to be conscious of time or her surroundings as the words flew from the typewriter.

At last it was done, and Lynsey had discovered that the man who had stood so fatefully between herself and Francis was none other than Dickon, Earl of Dartington, the man whom Henry had decided she was to marry. To whom Henry had sold her in marriage, in fact.

Almost too exhausted to move, Campion stood up and pushed away her typewriter. She ought to go upstairs. She felt as though she could sleep for a week, but she was just too tired to move and, besides, it was warm here in the kitchen. She curled up in the chair besides the fire, her body relaxing almost immediately into a deep sleep.

So deep, in fact, that she didn't hear the click of the restored lights, nor the car arriving outside, nor the opening of the back door.

Guy shook the sleet from his head and grimaced wearily. He seemed to have been driving round for a lifetime, trying to decide what to do—to go back to London or to stay. Perhaps he should have gone back, but in the end he couldn't. Too much hung on his being here, and he still wasn't sure if his decision was that of a fool or a coward.

He started to cross the kitchen, and then

frowned as he saw the typewriter on the table.

He walked over and touched the pages, turning them over and starting to read, slowly at first and then more quickly, his eyes narrowing as he pulled out a chair and sat down, no longer skimming through the typed pages, but reading them properly.

A small sound behind him broke his concentration. He turned in his chair, his eyes widening as he saw Campion.

She was curled up in her sleep, almost like a little girl with her hair tousled softly round her face, but she was no child, he reminded himself.

And then she moved in her sleep, and the illusion was destroyed as the fabric of her pyjama jacket pulled across her breasts. Heat crawled slowly through his skin, and he cursed bitterly under his breath.

What the hell was the matter with him? He frowned and started to turn deliberately away, but Campion moved again, stretching slightly in her sleep as though her body was cramped. She had very long legs and, as she stretched, her pyjama jacket rode up, revealing their slender, pale-skinned length.

He had had enough of this, Guy decided tormentedly. He walked over to the chair, and with one swift movement picked her up.

Her eyes opened and she stared into his face, and said sleepily, 'Dickon, what are you doing here?'

And then her eyes closed again and her face turned into his shoulder. He could feel the warmth of her breath against his skin, and he was breathing harshly by the time he reached her bedroom. He put her down on the bed and then started to pull the covers over her. A strand of her hair had curled round one of the buttons of his jacket, and he swore softly as he was forced to unravel it.

His hand shook, and he had to grit his teeth and force himself to concentrate. The buttons of her jacket gaped and he could see the soft swell of her breasts. At last he was free, and he straightened up tensely.

Back downstairs, he picked up the pages he hadn't finished reading. Dickon, she had called him. Of course, she would cast him as the villain. And then he read on, and stopped, a slow smile curling his mouth.

'So that was the way it was going to be, was it? Mmm . . . Very clever.'

When he had finished reading, he stacked the pages neatly together and found a piece of paper and a pen.

'Excellent, I like it,' he scribbled on it, and put the paper down on top of the manuscript.

When he went to bed, he took the stairs two at a time and whistled softly under his breath. Perhaps he had not made the wrong decision, after all. Perhaps . . .

He wondered if Campion would remember what she had said to him when she woke up. Somehow, he doubted it. He smiled again and opened his bedroom door.

CHAPTER FIVE

HOW had she got up here? Campion wondered muzzily as she opened her eyes. The last thing she remembered was crawling into the chair beside the fire.

She looked up and saw that the bedroom light was on. Well, at least the power had come back on. And then she remembered why she had worked until she was so exhausted that she could sleep.

Guy had gone.

A horrible empty feeling made her stomach cave hollowly, followed by a fierce flash of anger. She shouldn't be feeling like that. What was the matter with her? She should be glad that he had gone. But she wasn't. She shivered under the bedclothes and closed her eyes again, trying to fight the feeling of panic rising up inside her.

She didn't want to feel like this; there was no room in her life for this ridiculous, adolescent sort of emotion. What had happened to her will-power, to the years she had spent teaching herself how to stop herself from wanting . . .

From wanting what? Guy French in her life? In her arms . . . in her bed?

No!

The word was a silent protest that screamed painfully inside her. What was she trying to do to herself? Guy French didn't want her. How could he? All right, so he had passed her a couple of compliments. So what? That didn't mean that she had to over-react . . . like a woman who had deliberately repressed her sexuality for years and was now unable to repress it any longer.

Just thinking about him was enough to make her body tingle. To make her breasts ache and her body contract sharply. She was trembling as she flung back the covers and got out of bed.

Suddenly, she found it all too easy to understand Lynsey's rebellious emotions. If nothing else, Guy French was having a very definite effect on her work, she acknowledged grimly as she showered and then dressed.

The kitchen was blissfully warm. How on earth had the boiler managed to stay in? And surely she hadn't brought in that bucket of fuel last night?

Shaking her head at her own inability to remember, she filled the kettle. Outside, the wind seemed to have dropped and the rain had gone.

She was alone here as she had originally intended, but, instead of feeling triumph at having driven Guy away, she was intensely aware of her loneliness.

Why had she never acknowledged this feeling before? It had been there, only she had buried it so deeply that she had never allowed herself to recognise it. It was frightening how much she could miss Guy after such a very short space of time.

As she waited for the kettle to boil, her memory started to play unwanted tricks on her. As a teenager, she had longed for a husband and family of her own. With this mythical family, she would experience the love and security she had never felt with her own parents. But didn't all teenage girls go through that stage? she derided herself angrily. She had been lucky, she had discovered very early on in life how empty and meaningless marriage could be.

Lucky? To have had her hopes and dreams destroyed so cruelly, and with them all her burgeoning sexuality?

Stop it. Stop it! she warned herself fiercely. There was no point in going over and over the past. It had happened; that was a fact of life. She was what she was: a moderately intelligent woman who had been lucky enough to find she had a talent for writing and, in doing so, had discovered a means of escape from the grim reality of her loneliness.

The kettle boiled and switched itself off. Campion didn't notice. She was staring blankly at the wall. She *wasn't* lonely, she was solitary; it was a different thing. She had friends, very good friends . . .

So good, that none of them, apart from Lucy, knew about her past—about Craig. She shivered involuntarily. All right, so she didn't discuss Craig with anyone, but why should she? It was over, finished. And she had come to terms with what had happened years ago.

Had she? Then why did she feel like crying out for someone to tell her that Craig was wrong, that she was desirable? Why did she feel that her life was empty? Why did she ache for—for Guy French?

She shuddered and gripped the worktop. What on earth was she trying to do to herself? Guy would never want . . .

'Good, you're just putting the kettle on. I'm ready for a drink.'

Campion stared at the open doorway, and Guy, as though she had never seem him before in her

life. All the colour drained from her skin, leaving it
so pale that he frowned and instinctively took a
step towards her.

'Campion, are you all right?'

He was going to touch her and she couldn't let
him do that. Not now . . . Frantically, she backed
away from him and said huskily, 'You're back.'

'Yes, don't you remember? I came back last
night, having spent the evening driving round in
circles, trying to work off my temper.'

Last night. He had come back last night. She had
a vivid memory of her own surprise at waking up in
bed this morning, when she had known she had
fallen asleep in the chair. She fought to get hold of
another elusive and very worrying memory, but it
slipped from her.

'Miss me, did you?'

He was smiling at her, and her whole body
burned with pain and resentment. How dared he
pretend that he cared how she felt, one way or the
other? How dared he treat her in this mock
flirtatious manner, when they both knew he
couldn't possibly find her remotely attractive? It
was an insult to her intelligence. It was . . . She
fought to get a grip on herself, to stop herself from
betraying to him what she was feeling.

'As a matter of fact, I was too busy working to
miss you,' she told him coolly.

'Yes, so I noticed. I read what you'd done.
Didn't you see the note I left for you?'

He'd read her work, before she'd checked it
herself? The same hollow feeling she'd experienced
earlier came back, but this time it was stronger,
more painful.

'It's coming along nicely,' Guy continued,

apparently oblivious to her tension. 'Will she take him in the end?'

'Will who take whom?' Campion asked him, confused.

'Lynsey. Will she take Dickon? The King's choice.'

Campion had the uncomfortable feeling that there was more to the casual question than she could see.

'I don't know. I haven't decided yet.'

Guy was giving her an odd look, a mixture of exasperation and . . . tenderness. Tenderness? She looked away from him. She was letting her imagination go too far.

'Your Dickon's a very strong character,' Guy told her. 'Perhaps he won't give Lynsey much choice. Unlike me, he seems to have an overwhelming passion for small, high breasts . . .'

He was alluding to the passage she had written describing Dickon's awareness of her heroine, but, as he spoke, Guy was looking at *her* . . . at her body, Campion realised on a sudden flush of anger. He was looking at her breasts, surely hardly noticeable beneath her thick clothes. What was more, he was looking at her as though there was nothing he wanted more than to strip those clothes from her body and to take her breasts into his hands and . . .

What was she doing to herself? Her mind seemed to have devised its own cruel form of torment for her. She knew that there was no possibility of Guy looking at her with such yearning desire, and, if he was doing to, it could only be to taunt her . . . to mock her.

On a fiercely protective surve of rage, she retorted dangerously, 'Yes, I think everyone knows what you have a passion for.'

For a moment, Guy looked almost unsure of himself. Hard colour stung the high planes of his cheekbones, and then abruptly he was smiling at her, his smile loaded with mockery and malice.

'Do they? What?'

Now, when it was too late, she wished she hadn't been so quick to challenge him. Instead of responding, she shrugged her shoulders and turned her attention back to the kettle.

'If you're making breakfast, I'll have bacon, eggs and toast. But first I need a shower. I've just been out to check on the generator. If we have another power cut like last night's we'll need it.'

So he was staying. The relief that filled her also humiliated her. She had to turn away from him so that he wouldn't see it in her eyes. She wanted to tell him that he could make his own breakfast but, after all, yesterday he had made hers.

He was a very confusing man, she acknowledged as he went upstairs. Before, if she had given any thought to the matter, she would have considered him to be the type of man who expected the woman in his life to be subservient to him, to put him first in everything and to wait on him hand and foot. And yet, already he had demonstrated to her how wrong those preconceived ideas of hers were. He had tackled the household chores willingly, cheerfully and very ably, more ably than she had herself, she acknowledged fifteen minutes later, as she battled with the Rayburn's hotplates, so different from her own modern gas cooker.

Guy came down as she was staring miserably at the congealing and hard eggs she had just tried to cook.

She didn't hear him come in, and the unexpected weight of his hand on her shoulder as he leaned over to look into the pan made her jump. She turned quickly and saw him frown as his fingers investigated the narrowness of her bones beneath the thick padding of her clothes.

'You don't look after yourself properly,' he stunned her by saying. 'You're too thin.'

'I'm not thin, I'm slender,' she snapped at him. 'Not all men like women with curves like—like Marilyn Monroe.'

As she spoke, she had a vivid mental picture of the woman she had seen waiting for him in reception the last time she had visited the offices. She had been a stunningly curvaceous brunette, her figure encased in a clinging jersey outfit.

Her words had been purely defensive, and so she was surprised to see the anger flash suddenly and dangerously into Guy's eyes. His grip on her shoulder tightened, and irrationally she began to feel acutely vulnerable and frail. He wasn't a heavy man, but he was tall and broad and, from the pressure those fingers were exerting, a very fit man.

'What are you trying to say to me, Campion?' he asked bitingly. 'That I don't have the intelligence to respect a woman for what she is? Do you really think I'm the kind of man who looks for Barbie doll measurements in a woman and nothing else? Or don't you credit me with the sensitivity to see your insult for what it was? For your information, I like women—all kinds of women; but what I find most attractive and exciting about them is their personalities.'

He was lying to her. She had seen the women he dated.

He was looking away from her now and into the pan.

'Mind you,' he added with a grin, 'it does help if they can cook . . . What *is* this?'

He prodded her cast-iron eggs with the fork, and Campion glared up at him.

'Mm . . . not exactly easy-over, are they?'

To her horror, instead of snapping back at him, Campion felt tears begin to sting her eyes.

It was years since she had cried, aeons ago . . . She never gave way to feminine emotion, and yet here she was, ready to burst into tears simply because a man criticised her cooking.

Even as she derided herself for her weakness, she acknowledged that it wasn't really the eggs; they were simply the thing on which her emotions had focused.

What she wanted to cry for was the destruction of her womanliness, for the fates that had been so cruel in forming her as a woman who ached and yearned to form a loving bond with a man she could want and respect, and yet whose outward physical appearance made it impossible.

Through a blur of tears, she saw Guy move away from her. Her body felt cold, as though it had enjoyed the warmth of the proximity of his. She was humiliating herself, dissolving into tears in front of him like this. He would be embarrassed and uncomfortable. Men always were when women cried.

She remembered how her mother had cautioned her not to give in to her tears after Craig had told her what he really felt for her. It would upset her father, her mother had told her. Men did not like tears. Tears were a weapon that women used to get their own way, and which men quite rightly resented.

Campion had turned her head away the moment

she felt the betraying prickle at the back of her eyes, but she couldn't see anything. The kitchen was a watery blur. All her concentrating went into trying to control her emotions.

'Hey, it's all right. Come and sit down.'

She froze as she felt Guy's hands on her shoulders, gently propelling her to the table and pushing her down into a chair.

'Come on, have a good howl, and then you'll feel better.'

A soft white handkerchief was pressed expertly against her face, and it took her several seconds to overcome her shock and take hold of it for herself.

'I never cry.'

What on earth had she said that for?

'Then you should. Women who don't cry throw things.'

She put down the handkerchief and stared at him.

'It's a way of releasing tension.'

Guy was sitting on the edge of the table, looking at her. There was such a tender look in his eyes that she blinked, and then blinked again when it didn't disappear.

'Why is it you're so desperately afraid of showing emotion, Campion? You're going through a very stressful time,' he added quietly when she made no response. 'There's no reason for you to feel ashamed because . . .'

'Because I can't fry eggs,' she interrupted savagely.

To her fury, he laughed. 'Ah, well, that's another story. Using a Rayburn takes a bit of know-how . . . Want me to show you?'

She didn't want him to show her anything. She

wanted him to leave her alone and free her from the dangerous spell of his intimacy. He was reacting to her in a way that was totally unfamiliar to her; treating her . . . treating her as a woman, she recognised with a quick start.

'Who taught you?' she asked coldly. 'One of your women?'

He didn't like that, and no wonder. She saw the tenderness fade from his eyes, to be replaced with a cool sternness that made her quail slightly.

'No, as a matter of fact, my mother taught me,' he said quietly.

'Your mother?'

'Yes. I was her eldest child. My father died when I was twelve, and Ma had to go out to work. She taught me to cook, so that I could prepare a meal for the others when we got home from school.'

'The others?'

He smiled then, and it was a smile she couldn't wholly interpret; she saw that it held love and resignation, and other things as well, and she was pierced with a pain that was compounded of loss and envy and a terrible, aching unhappiness that she knew nothing in her life would ever totally dim.

She loved him . . . She loved this intelligent, beautiful man who had women falling over themselves to attract his attention. She loved him, and part of her twisted in mortal agony that she could be so foolish and so vulnerable.

It hadn't happened overnight. It had to have been there for some time, growing slowly and dangerously. This time together at the cottage had acted like a forcing house, making her recognise what was happening to her.

Before, she had been able to ignore the insidious growth of her feelings, pretending that her awareness of him sprang from dislike and resentment; here, at the cottage, there was no barrier behind which she could hide from the truth. She loved him.

'My sisters and brother,' he told her softly.

She turned away quickly so that he wouldn't see her envy. She had hated being an only child; had longed for the companionship that came from being part of a family. Perhaps she had even turned to Craig out of that need.

'You have sisters and a brother?'

'I certainly do. Alison and Meg are twins; they're three years younger than me, and Ian is the baby of the family. He had just started school when Pa was killed. It was a wrench for Ma to leave him and go back to work. She lost the baby she was carrying when my father died.'

'What—what happened to him?' Campion asked, barely aware of saying the words.

It amazed her that he could talk to her like this. She never discussed her private past life with anyone.

'He was killed by a hit-and-run driver two days before Christmas.'

Champion turned an appalled face towards him.

'*Christmas*! How dreadful . . .'

'I can see what you're thinking, and you're wrong,' he told her quietly. 'Of course, we never forgot, but Ma never allowed the spirit of Christmas to be damaged for us by Pa's death. They were two separate things, and she treated them as such. She still does.'

'Where—where does she live?'

'In Dorset, close to the girls. They're both married now, with families. Ian is working in Canada . . . What about you?' he asked, deftly removing the eggs from the pan he had put down on the table.

'Me?'

'Yes, you. Do you have a large family . . . brothers—sisters?'

'No.' Her voice sounded oddly harsh and she took a deep, steadying breath, and said less forcefully, 'No, I was an only one. My parents died some time ago.'

'An only one. You must have been very lonely.'

She wanted to deny it, but the words clogged her throat.

'Come on,' he added, smiling at her. 'Here beginneth your first lesson in the correct use of a Rayburn cooker.'

Bemused, Campion allowed him to lead her back to the stove. Silently, she watched his easy movements, and listened as he instructed her.

'Ma brought us all up to be self-sufficient. We had to be. My father was insured, but that only paid for the house.'

This time, the eggs were cooked perfectly, but Campion couldn't eat hers.

In the space of a few minutes, her whole world had turned upside-down. How could she have dared to love Guy? How could she have been so stupid?

Guy made the coffee, and watched her as she sat, motionless, staring into space.

'Something's wrong,' he said quietly. 'Want to talk about it?'

To *talk* about it? What on earth could she say?

I've just discovered that I love you?

'It's nothing. I was just thinking about the book.'

She saw the shadow cross his face, and for a moment he almost looked rebuffed, as though she had somehow hurt him.

Wishful thinking, she told herself as she got up awkwardly. 'I'd better go and make a start.'

He didn't follow her, and she should have felt easier without his presence, but the words just wouldn't flow. She sat and stared at the typewriter, without seeing anything.

'Mental block?'

She hadn't heard him come in.

'I . . .'

He picked up the manuscript.

'She's a lot like you, isn't she? Remote . . . alone . . .'

'Like *me*?' Campion shook, as she said bitterly, 'No, she's nothing like me. For one thing, she's beautiful, while I . . .'

'While you do everything you can to deny that you're a woman,' Guy interrupted calmly. 'But you *are* a woman, Campion.'

What was he trying to do to her? Didn't he realise how frighteningly vulnerable she was? Why was he looking at her like that, as though—as though——?

'Oh, I know you do everything you can to deny your feminity. Scrape back your hair, disguise your body . . .'

'What am I suppose to do?' she demanded, suddenly losing control of her feelings. 'Deck myself out in make-up and alluring clothes, in the hope that a man might come along who's deceived into thinking that I'm actually desirable? Don't you think I have more pride than to . . .'

'What the hell are you talking about?' Guy interrupted flatly. 'You are desirable.'

What was he trying to do to her?

'No. No, I'm not.' She saw the way he looked at her, and laughed harshly. 'Don't you think that I wish I was? I know the truth, Guy. I had it pointed out to me and underlined quite plainly when I was nineteen.'

'How?'

She stared at him, shocked into silence by his question. How had they got to this point? How had she been stupid enough to betray so much to him?

She looked round the small room, seeking an escape.

'You tell me that you aren't desirable. Well, I'm telling you that you are. Would you like me to show you just how much I want you, Campion? When I carried you up to bed last night, I wanted to stay with you. The reason I walked out last night was because I couldn't trust myself to stay. I look at you and I ache to touch you, to make love to you.'

'No! No, I won't listen. You're lying to me. Craig——'

'Craig,' he pounced, watching her. 'Who's Craig?'

She was shivering with a mixture of shock and pain, but he made no attempt to touch her, to comfort her.

'My—my ex-husband . . .'

She had surprised him now. She saw it in his face; in the way he suddenly went very still, his gaze sharpening and hardening slightly.

'You've been married . . .'

Suddenly, she picked up his thoughts.

'What did you think? That I was still virginal and inexperienced?' she asked bitterly. 'At my age? Yes, I've been married. I was married when I was nineteen.'

'And when did you and your husband part?'

She thought about lying to him, but dismissed the notion and said tiredly, 'A week after we were married. He didn't want me. He just wanted my parents' money, and once he realised that it wouldn't be forthcoming he couldn't wait to get rid of me.'

'You'd been lovers . . .'

'Yes. Before we were married, we—he made love to me. He told me he thought I might be pregnant. I believed him, and so we ran away and got married.' She shrugged. 'I was very young . . . very naïve.'

'And because of this—this man, you really believe that you're undesirable? Because one man——' he began incredulously. 'I don't believe I'm hearing this!'

'No, Craig made me see the truth, that's all. I'm just not the kind of woman that men desire.' She wasn't going to repeat the insults and taunts that Craig had thrown at her; words that she could never forget, wounds that would never heal.

'I don't want to talk about it any more. I've got work to do.'

'Because of *one* man, you're going to shut the rest of the male sex out of your life, is that it? Because you're afraid . . .'

He was going to touch her. Campion could sense it, and suddenly she was panic-stricken. If he did . . .

She stood up abruptly, pushing past him, ignoring him as he called out her name. She had to get away. She had to be on her own. Her mind and emotions were in such turmoil.

He caught up with her in the kitchen.

'I'm going for a walk. I want to be on my own.'

Perhaps something in her face warned him not to touch her, because he stepped back slightly.

'All right, if that's what you want, but you're wrong, you know, Campion. And he was wrong, too . . .'

As she pulled on her boots, she turned on him, her expression fierce and proud.

'I'm not a fool, Guy, not any more. I realise that flirting comes as naturally to you as breathing, but that doesn't disguise the truth. Physically, men find me repellant. I know that, and no amount of you pretending it isn't true is going to change things.'

He looked angry now, really angry. He came up to her and grabbed hold of her arm so that she almost fell over. Instinctively, she clung on to him, and then wished she hadn't as her senses were over-whelmed by the nearness of him. She started to shake, but he seemed unaware of her vulnerability. His grip on her arm tightened as he looked down into her face.

'Do you know what I think?' he said softly. 'I think you're a coward, Campion. I think you're afraid. Afraid of living, afraid of loving, afraid of . . . And so you've shut yourself away behind a wall of pride and resentment. So you made a mistake, an error of judgement . . . Don't you think we *all* make those mistakes at one time or another? But the rest of us have the guts to pick ourselves up and go on with life. It isn't desirability you lack,' he added in disgust. 'It's guts.'

'Really!' The smile she gave him felt as though it was pasted on her face. 'Haven't you left something out?'

She watched as he frowned.

'You haven't told me yet that I'm frigid,' she added bitterly. 'That *is* what you were going to say next, isn't it?'

Before he could say anything, she pulled out of his grasp and opened the back door.

This was the second time she had run from him like this. Her heart thudded painfully in her chest, although she knew without looking over her shoulder that he wasn't following her.

Oh, God, what had she done? What had she said? Why hadn't she kept quiet? Why had she allowed him to needle her into betraying so much?

How could she ever face him again? She started to shiver.

She couldn't go back. He was an intelligent man. When he had time to think over what she had said, what was there to stop him from guessing how she really felt?

She stumbled on, sliding on the muddy path, turning instinctively towards the coast.

The cliffs on the headland were steep, and the home for a variety of sea birds. The wind coming off the sea was still quite strong. She had walked blindly while she was angry, but now her anger had gone and reaction was setting in. She couldn't go back to the cottage. How could she face Guy?

She sat down on the wet grass and stared out to sea. Why had he said that he desired her? Probably out of some misguided attempt to flatter her. He couldn't have realised the avalanche of emotion his words would release, and he was probably feeling as battered as she was herself. She ought to go back and make her peace with him, but she couldn't.

~ She got up, shivering in the cold wind. A bird screeched mockingly overhead, and as she looked up it seemed to dive towards her. She ducked instinctively, and cried out as she felt herself slipping.

She fell heavily, but, instead of solid ground beneath her, she felt the earth moving, sliding, taking her with it as it broke away.

She knew that she screamed, but the sound was lost among the wild cries of the sea birds disturbed by the small avalanche.

Quite a large piece of the cliff had fallen away, and she had fallen with it. Below her she could see the foam-capped waves; above her was the clifftop. She was perched on less than four square feet of rock and earth that was somehow wedged between a rocky outcrop six feet below the top of the cliff.

Six feet, that was all, but it might just as well have been sixty. There was no way she could clamber up that almost vertical rock-face and back to safety. In fact, she dared not even move, terrified in case she destroyed her fragile security.

It had started to rain again, and surely the wind was harsher, buffeting against the cliff-face.

Gulls cried and swooped, and far out to sea she could see the grey outline of a boat. She dared not look down. She had always had a thing about water combined with height. If she looked, she would be drawn downwards, she knew it. She shivered, her jacket no protection against the wind and rain. And then, incredibly, she heard Guy's voice.

He was calling her name, his voice harsh.

Less than ten minutes ago she had felt she could never face him again, and yet now she woud have given anything to get up and run towards him.

It was several seconds before she could call out to him, and then several more before she could hear his voice again. Closer this time.

'I'm here, Guy. There was a landslide, the cliff . . . Be careful!' She stopped as she saw him looking down at her.

It must be the cold that was making him look so tense, as though at any second he feared his control might shatter.

'I think you'll have to go to the village to get help.'

He looked away from her, and she thought he said something, but she couldn't quite hear.

He disappeared completely then and, even though she knew he had to leave her to get help, she felt more abandoned than she had felt when her parents died, more alone than at any other time in her life.

Her ankle had gone numb and she moved instinctively, tensing abruptly as she felt her perch begin to tilt.

She had a momentary and unwanted view of the rocks below her, and the sea frothing angrily around the rocks, throwing up showers of grey-white spume. The tide was coming in. It couldn't reach her up here of course.

She shivered and bit down hard on her bottom lip. What was the point in crying now? It was her own folly that had brought her here. Her own crazy stupidity . . .

'Campion!'

She stared up at Guy. He hadn't left her, after all. He was leaning over the edge of the cliff. He must be lying flat on the ground, she recognised.

'I'm going to pass my jeans down to you. I want you to hold on to them as tightly as you can. I'm going to use them to pull you back up the cliff.'

Her mouth went dry. She wanted to refuse; what he was suggesting was madness! He was a very fit man, but she was no lightweight, and what he was suggesting could mean them both plummeting down on to those viciously sharp rocks and that icy-cold sea.

'Stand up slowly and carefully.'

Incredibly, she found she was doing as he told her and, even more incredibly, beneath her fear she felt a calmness, a sense of trust so new to her that she paused for a moment to marvel at it. Fear obviously bred strange emotions. Very strange emotions.

'Now, get hold of my jeans. Hold the fabric tightly, wrap it round your wrists. Yes, that's it.'

Panic flared inside her, but she fought it down.

'Now, I want you to put your feet as flat as you can against the cliff-face . . .'

He wanted her to *what?* She felt sick at the thought of what he was suggesting. She couldn't do it. If she even tried, she would fall.

'You've got to do it, Campion.'

Was that desperation she heard in his voice? She looked up at him, and then gasped as she felt her small island of security tilt a little further.

'*Now!* You've got to do it now.'

She heard the skitter of rocks as they fell away beneath her, and perhaps it was that that gave her the courage to move, or perhaps it was the sheer strength of Guy's voice, she didn't know, but suddenly she was stepping off her perch, placing her feet as he had told her, leaning out slightly, gripping the denim fabric until her arms ached, as Guy slowly pulled her up the cliff-face.

All she could do to help him was to gain a little extra leverage by using her feet. Her fear for herself vanished as, slowly, inch by inch, he pulled her to safety, and all she could think was that, if she didn't do all she could to help him, she could fall, and take Guy himself with her. And then, unbelievably, her eyes were on a level with the top of the cliff.

'Hold on,' Guy instructed her tersely.

It was bliss to feel the cold, wet grass against her skin as Guy pulled her the last few feet to safety, before grabbing hold of her and dragging them both well back from the cliff edge.

'You saved my life!'

He was kneeling on the ground beside her, breathing harshly as his body reacted to the strain.

She wanted to reach out to him and hold him, to tell him that he was right and that she was a coward, but even as she moved she saw his face close up and an icy coldness filled her. She *had* been right, after all. She hadn't missed that brief but unmistakable movement away from her just then. He had lied to her. He didn't desire her, and she was a fool for ever letting herself think he might.

She started to stand up. Her whole body threatened to buckle under the efforts, but she was too proud to let Guy see how she felt. He had just shown her how he felt about the thought of any physical contact between them.

'Come on, let's get back to the cottage. It's going to start pouring down.'

They should have looked idiotic. A woman almost plastered in mud all down her front, and a man wearing a thick shirt, a heavy sweater, briefs and socks, but Campion didn't care how they looked. Guy had saved her life, but for . . . Reaction started to set in. She was shivering . . . She looked instinctively at Guy, but he turned away, his face bleak.

CHAPTER SIX

'WE COULD both do with a bath,' Guy announced, grimacing in self-disgust once they were safely inside the kitchen.

He hadn't said a word during the cold, wet walk back to the cottage. How had he known where to find her? Campion wondered as she stood and shivered. How had he known she even needed help?

'You go first,' she offered awkwardly.

'I can manage down here.'

Again that harsh tone. Her muscles tensed as she recognised that he was avoiding looking directly at her. Why? Was it because of their discussion earlier, or because of the way she had reached out towards him. Had it suddenly struck him that she might take his words seriously, that she might think he was actually attracted to her? Did he really think she was so stupid?

'Upstairs, Campion. Unless, of course, you get a thrill out of watching men strip off.'

Her skin burned. He couldn't have thought of a more cruel way to taunt her.

All the way back she had avoided looking at his body, but now she couldn't help it. She could feel the heat burning up under her skin as he turned his back on her and deliberately started to remove his sweater and shirt. Her mouth went dry. She ached to be able to reach out and touch him, to see if his skin felt as warm and male as it looked. And then she realised that Guy was turning round.

With a small, choked cry, she fled upstairs.

She had a bath, washed her hair, dried it as best she could with a towel, grimacing at the tangle of curls that hung on to her shoulders. Pulling on her bathrobe, she gathered up her wet clothes and headed back to her bedroom.

As she walked in, she saw that Guy was standing with his back to her, staring out of the window. Like her, he was dressed in a towelling robe. His legs beneath its short hem were bare and brown. Her own toes curled protestingly into the carpet. She didn't want to see him like this. It made it all so much harder.

He turned round abruptly and stared at her, and instinctively she tugged at her robe and wished that she had been able to do something more sensible with her hair.

'We have to talk . . .'

Of course. She ought to have expected that.

'There's nothing to talk about, Guy,' she said wearily. 'You needn't worry. I didn't take what you said seriously.'

A muscle twitched in his jaw.

'Like hell! You took it seriously enough to walk out of here and damn well nearly kill yourself.'

Kill herself? Did he actually think . . .?

'That was an accident. I walked out in a temper, I admit, but you don't think I actually . . .'

Guy pushed his hand into his hair. He looked tired.

'No, no, of course not. But you must see that we can't go on like this. I think it would be best if I left . . .'

Oh, God! But wasn't it what she had been expecting? For the sake of her pride, if nothing else, she mustn't let him see how she felt; she mustn't let him guess at the pain exploding inside her. She opened her mouth to make a cool, composed response and then, to her horror, she heard herself crying out bitterly, 'Do you really think I'm so much of a fool that I believed you, Guy? Did you honestly think I had deluded myself into believing that you wanted me? You're quite safe, you know. I never had any intention of asking you to prove that you weren't lying.'

'What . . .'

He was looking at her rather strangely, with a different grimness round his mouth, and a glimmer of something in the back of his eyes that made her stomach kick dangerously.

'Just what in hell are you talking about? You may not be a fool, but you certainly have the lowest self-esteem of any woman I've ever met.'

The softness in his voice unnerved her. He had turned round and was watching her, and she had the curious sensation of being trapped and defenceless.

'I'd hardly call it low self-esteem to realise that an attractive, virile man is extremely unlikely to be consumed with desire for me,' she said proudly, determined not to let him see how much the admission hurt.

'Then what would you call it?' Guy demanded, without taking his eyes off her face.

'Reality,' she told him firmly. 'You said you were going to leave . . .' She wanted him to go quickly, before she broke down and begged him to stay. If she did that . . . She tried to breathe, and felt her whole body quiver with pain.

She turned her back on him, and so it was a shock

to feel his hands on her arms, dragging her round to face him. He was breathing hard, as though he had been running. And he looked angry, furiously angry. Her heart kicked in her chest, and she shivered beneath a frisson of sexual need.

'That was before,' he told her cryptically. 'God, Campion, I've never known a woman like you. Have you really no idea what you are, what you're *doing* to me? All this time . . . At first I thought——' He shook his head and continued after a pause. 'There has to be a way to get through to you.'

Still holding on to her, he looked round the room. Before she could protest, Campion found herself dragged in front of an old-fashioned Victorian pier-glass which threw back to her their full-length reflections. He dwarfed her in height and in breadth. He made her look small and frail. With her hair tumbling around her shoulders, she looked different, even to herself.

'Look at yourself,' he commanded her huskily, dragging the robe from her body, exposing her nudity, not just to his gaze, but also to her own. Before she could react, before she could cry out in protest, he was shrugging off his own robe.

'Look at *us*,' he demanded softly. 'And look at what you do to *me*.'

He stood without touching her, watching the colour crawl up under her skin as she hurriedly looked away from the open arousal of his body.

'*This* is reality,' he told her. 'This is the way you make me react, the way you make me feel. You say you're undesirable. To whom? A man without grace or intelligence, who once hurt you badly? Have you any idea how insulting I find it to be classed with him? Have you any idea of how angry you make me

when you tell me that you aren't desirable? Have you
any idea of how much you make me ache and long to
take hold of you and show you just how wrong you
are? I want you, Campion, and I think you want me,
too.'

He was turning away from the mirror and towards
her.

'No! No, I . . .'

'Yes.' His voice, thick and oddly muffled, made
Campion's mind spin. She felt his mouth touch her
skin, not teasingly or lightly as she had expected, but
hungrily, fiercely, like a man out of control. She
shuddered beneath its pressure, her throat arching
back, her body absorbing the heat of his. She could
feel the furious thud of his heart, and her own started
to race in time to it. She moaned as his mouth
savaged her throat. This was nothing like how she
had imagined it might be. She had visualised him as a
controlled, even distant lover, but there was nothing
in the least controlled or distant about the way he was
touching her. He shuddered against her and moaned
her name against her skin. Somehow or other, her
arms had tightened around him. Her breasts were
pressed against his chest and, as he moved, it created
a delicious friction against their tender peaks.

His hands moved over her, shaping her body,
making her ache to touch him in turn. His mouth had
reached her jawline now. She turned her head, her
eyes wide and dark with arousal.

'Kiss me. Kiss me, Guy . . .'

She wasn't aware of saying the words, only of the
feverish need building inside her.

He lifted his head, his hands cupping her face, his
skin flushed with dark colour.

'Oh, my God, yes. This is how I've wanted to see

you. This is how I've wanted to make you feel.' His lips touched hers, and she trembled. She felt Guy's body tense, then his head lifted again so that she was denied the contact she craved. She opened the eyes she had closed in anticipation of the pleasure of having his mouth on hers.

He was staring down at her.

'Open your mouth, so that I can kiss you properly . . .'

In a dream, she obeyed his command. It was nothing like the kisses she had experienced with Craig. Kisses which, if she was honest, had not really moved her at all. With Guy, it was different. Her whole body seemed to melt beneath the heat of his touch.

She felt him lift her, and marvelled absently at his strength; she felt the coolness of the bedclothes against her naked back, and the warmth of Guy's weight as he took her back into his arms.

He kissed her again, lingeringly this time, as though she was a rare delight that had to be savoured, and she responded eagerly, hungrily to his touch, barely aware of the way she was caressing the naked length of his spine until he groaned against her mouth, unable to control the fierce thrusting movement of his body.

'I wanted to do this slowly, to make it special for you, but you're making it impossible for me to think of anything but how much I want you.'

Campion shivered, the words arousing her almost as much as his touch. This was a dream, it had to be, and she gave herself up to the pleasure of it voluptuously, arching her body sinuously to Guy's touch, feeling pleasure and power flow through her as he responded to her allure.

'You're beautiful, even more beautiful that I'd imagined.' His hand cupped her breast, and Campion tensed for a moment as he looked down at her, to where his hand lay against the paleness of her own flesh.

'Beautiful,' he repeated huskily, and Campion gasped as he bent his head and took her nipple into his mouth.

She had never experienced a sensation like it. Her whole body convulsed on a wave of feeling so strong that, for a moment, it almost frightened her.

A woman's instinct she had not known she possessed told her that Guy was dangerously close to losing control. She touched him tentatively, stroking the narrow curve of his hip and the flat plane of his belly. She felt the harsh rasp of hair against her fingertips. It was an electrifying sensation. Instinctively, her fingers drifted downwards, and then stilled as she realised just what she was doing.

'My God! What is it you're trying to do to me?'

She froze as she heard the harsh, almost anguished words. Guy moved, looking down at her. He looked angry, and she shivered, all her old uncertainties sweeping back. She had hurt him somehow, done something he didn't like. She felt confused and ignorant. It was ridiculous at her age to know so little about male sexuality. Craig had never encouraged her to touch him.

'I—I didn't mean to hurt you . . .'

Tears weren't far away, but she fought them back.

'*Hurt* me?' She could feel Guy's tension. He muttered something under his breath, and she felt her skin almost hurt with embarrassment. Then suddenly the tension seemed to leave him, and his hands were moving over her body, stroking her, caressing her, catching her up in a tide of sensation that allowed her to do nothing other than feel.

She felt the arousing stroke of Guy's fingers against her inner thigh, and she held her breath, aching with an unfamiliar tension, an unknown need. She wanted . . . She gasped in protest as his hand moved away and then touched her again. She could feel his mouth moving softly against her shoulder, but neither sensation was what she wanted. She wanted . . . Her body started to shake, her throat tight with the effort of controlling the soft moans of need she was having to suppress. She moved, trying to tell Guy without words what it was she wanted, but he seemed oblivious to her need.

Then, so suddenly that it was almost shocking, he released her, bracing his hands flat against the bed on either side of her as he said quietly, 'You weren't *hurting* me, Campion; at least, not the way you meant. *That* was what you were doing to me—what I was just doing to you.'

She stared up at him, not knowing what to say, and then humiliation overwhelmed her. What kind of woman was she that she didn't even know, that she had to be shown . . . She made a tiny sound of self-disgust and tried to turn away, but Guy wouldn't let her.

He took her back in his arms and stroked her sensitive skin until she was pleading with him in breathless, husky whispers to end her torment, reaching out for him, touching him, sobbing in a mixture of triumph and release as he cried out her name and finally let go of the control he had used to keep them both in check.

She tensed briefly as he entered her, but there was no pain, no fear; only a wonderful feeling of

rightness, of relief and then of dazzling joy as she
became aware of her body's instinctive response to
his powerful thrusts.

What began as the smallest trickle of sensation
built up so quickly that its climax took her by
surprise: a fierce storm of sensation that made Guy
cry out her name as he lost himself completely within
her.

She felt the release of his body within her own, felt
it and rejoiced in it with a primitive sense of power
she had not known existed. Her body ached, but it
was a pleasurable ache, a triumphant ache. She felt
Guy leave her, and her flesh grew chilled, but he was
simply pulling the bedclothes back over them, his
body cushioning hers, warming it, cherishing it.

She drifted off to sleep on that thought.

When Campion woke up it was dark, and she was so
thoroughly disorientated that for a moment she
could barely remember *who* she was, let alone where.
Guy lay sleeping beside her. She turned her head to
look at him. Her insides quivered and melted, and
then surged with quickening desire.

She quelled the sensation, disconcerted by her own
sexuality, but the tiny, burgeoning ache refused to go
away. Was this how Lynsey would have felt? Or
would she have been angry with herself for allowing
herself to feel like this for a man whom she felt she
hated? She would not have expected to find such
pleasure in her marriage bed, and she would resent its
discovery and the power it gave Dickon over her.

Silently, Campion got out of bed and found her
robe. Ten minutes later she was downstairs, typing
furiously, lost in her work. So lost, in fact, that she
didn't even hear Guy coming downstairs himself.

He asked wryly, half an hour later, 'Can I interrupt?'

She almost jumped in shock.

'If this is the effect making love with me has on you, I can see we're going to have to do it more often.'

He was teasing her, she knew, and she was grateful to him for lightening what could have been a very difficult moment.

'Why did you sneak out of bed like that?'

She looked at him. 'I thought you were asleep. I didn't want to disturb you.'

The way he looked at her made her blush, and he laughed when he saw it.

'I don't suppose I can tempt you away from that typewriter for long enough to show you exactly how much you *do* disturb me, can I?'

For one crazy moment, she actually contemplated getting up. What on earth had he done to her?

'I . . . I really ought to finish this.'

'Yes, I know.' He bent down and, to her shock, she felt his lips move against her neck. A pulse point started to thud beneath his mouth. She badly wanted to turn to him and let him know how he was making her feel, but she was still too unsure of herself, still too new to such sensations to feel entirely comfortable with them.

'I . . . I suppose we ought to be thinking about something to eat . . .'

'Right now, what I want to eat is you.'

The words shivered across her skin, conjuring up images that made her feel weak and dizzy. Unlike her, Guy had dressed, and when he looked at her she felt acutely conscious of her nudity beneath her robe, but she had been so anxious to get to her typewriter that she hadn't even thought about getting dressed.

'You frightened me to death this afternoon. Do you realise that? If I'd lost you . . .'

The anguish in his voice shocked her. She turned her head to look at him, and something elusive and haunting in his eyes vanished, as though he didn't want her to see his feelings.

'I tell you what, I'll make dinner, but first you have to pay a forfeit.'

'What? Promise to wash up?'

—'That wasn't *quite* what I had in mind.'

The way he looked at her as he drew her to her feet made her insides turn over. As he bent his head to kiss her, his hand slid inside her robe. The sensation of his fingers against her breast and then her nipple made her moan softly beneath his kiss. Instantly, his touch hardened, demanded, and just as instantly she responded to it, aching to feel the hard strength of his body against her, aching to experience again that delicate rapture she had never known existed.

She wanted to cling to him when he realeased her but, instead, reluctantly she opened her eyes and looked up at him.

'This isn't going to get the dinner cooked, is it?' he said ruefully. 'You have a very undermining effect on my self-control; you're a very dangerous woman.'

A dangerous woman. She smiled to herself when he had gone. If she was a dangerous woman, then what did that make him?

From somewhere or other, Guy had found candles— only plain white kitchen ones, but he lit them with a flourish worthy of the most expensive and intimate restaurant and, as she sat down on the chair he pulled out for her, Campion marvelled at the versatility of this man whom she had originally dismissed as a lightweight chauvinist.

He had cooked a chicken casserole, and its succulent fragrance filled the room, but it was the sight of the wine bottle on the table that made her eyebrows lift in silent interrogation.

'I had to go down to the village. Champagne would have been more appropriate, but the off-licence doesn't stock it.'

He grinned at her and she smiled back. The off-licence was a tiny row of shelves in the cluttered general store that was the only retail outlet the village possessed, besides the chemist's shop and the launderette.

'I feel I should have made more of an effort to dress up.' Campion touched her hair awkwardly. She wasn't used to this feeling of wanting to please someone, of almost needing to see that slow, warm smile that began at the back of Guy's eyes and spread until his whole face was illuminated by it.

'I like you just the way you are.'

Incredibly, she could almost believe he meant it, and she gave a soft gurgle of amusement.

Once, long, long ago, she had tried to dress to please a man. Her face clouded as she remembered.

'Don't think about him,' Guy demanded tersely. 'He and I are two different men, Campion, and I don't like it when you compare us.'

'I wasn't.'

'There's been no one since, has there?' he questioned abruptly, as though he already knew the answer.

'No.' She looked away from him. 'I must seem very naïve, very inexperienced.' She pulled a face. 'Attractive in a very young woman, perhaps, but not so attractive in someone my age.'

She bit her lip and winced as he took hold of her abruptly.

'*Will* you stop doing that?'

She stared at him, hurt by the rough anger in his voice.

'Doing what?'

'Running yourself down,' he told her curtly. 'Experience doesn't guarantee physical pleasure.'

'I didn't even know how . . . how to touch you.' Her face flamed as she looked briefly at him. 'That was what was missing from my book, wasn't it?' she asked, suddenly illuminatingly aware of what had been behind his cricitisms. 'Knowledge . . . experience . . .'

'Sort of, but it was the emotional impact I was looking for, not the physical.' His hand touched her face, and instantly she quivered in response. Immediately, his eyes darkened and the breath stopped in her throat. 'Keep on looking at me like that, and we'll be eating this chicken for breakfast,' Guy told her ruefully.

It broke the tension. She laughed and watched, loving him as the smile broke out across his face.

How could she have not known before now that she loved him? She shivered, suddenly aware of how fleeting this precious time with him might be. He had said nothing of love, nothing of permanence, nothing of anything more than the fact that he wanted her.

'Come on, let's eat.'

He made her sit down, while he served the meal and then filled her wineglass.

Over dinner they talked, their conversation covering a wide diversity of subjects. He was entertaining to talk to, and a generous listener,

Campion discovered, as the wine relaxed her and she told him about the loneliness of her childhood and the horror of Craig's deceit.

'I envy you coming from such a large family,' she confessed. 'Do you see much of them?'

'Not as much as I'd like. I normally spend Christmas with Ma, but this year she's going to Canada. Ian has just got engaged, and of course he wants her to meet his fiancée and her family.'

'So you're the only one who's not married?'

Her face burned as she realised what she had just said.

'By accident, rather that choice.' The look he gave her was direct and firm. 'I was engaged briefly when I was twenty-two, but she changed her mind when she realised how long it would be before we could marry. I couldn't leave Ma to cope on her own. Ian was still at school at the time, and the girls just about to start university. Don't look like that. It wouldn't have worked anyway . . .'

She couldn't tell him that the tears shimmering in her eyes were for own stupidity in so nearly denying herself this precious time with him. He was such a very special man, and she was still marvelling that he could actually want her. Beautiful, he had called her, and he had touched her body with slow reverence, as though he did indeed find it worthy of such worship.

'No pudding, I'm afraid.'

'I couldn't eat another morsel,' she told him, and it was true. She ached to be back in his arms, wanted only the voluptuous, heady delight of feeling his skin against her own. Perhaps it was the wine that had brought on this feeling of wantonness, or perhaps it had always bee there, buried deep inside her, waiting for his touch to release it.

'Coffee?'

'Please.' She had to get herself under control. Guy might not want to make love to her again so soon . . .

'I thought we might go over the work I did this afternoon . . .' Her voice shook slightly, and she wondered if he could detect how she was really feeling.

'Fine. Coffee in the sitting-room, then?'

'I ought to make it. You made dinner.'

'You can make breakfast in the morning, instead.'

Her heart missed a beat, and she found that she couldn't look at him. Breakfast. Would he spend the night with her? Would he . . . her body went hot with desire, while her mind shrank from the intensity of her feelings. Instead of easing her need for him, their lovemaking only seemed to have increased it.

When he came in with the coffee, her head was bent over the newly typed pages, but she wasn't reading them.

She passed them over to him, and watched as he sat down. He read them quickly and thoroughly, pausing every now and again to re-read a few lines. Tension invaded her. What if it wasn't any good? What if the re-writes were every bit as unsatisfactory as her initial attempt? She had found this afternoon that she was no longer able to judge her own work; all she could do was to pass on to Lynsey her own feelings and experiences.

'That's good,' he said quietly when he had finished. 'Now I really feel that Lynsey is alive. I like the way she reacts to Dickon, the way she fights against her physical desire for him and tries to deny it. It makes an interesting point of conflict. You get very involved with your characters, don't you?' he asked softly.

For no reason at all, her throat had gone dry.

'Well, yes. I suppose I do. But what makes you say so?'

'The other night, when you fell asleep in the chair, when I picked you up and carried you upstairs, you called me Dickon.'

All at once she remembered that elusive, nagging sense of unease. Her face burned and she wanted desperately to look away from him.

'Don't be embarrassed. I like knowing that our lovemaking inspired you to write like this. In fact, I find it very arousing to know that I gave you so much pleasure. I *did* give you pleasure, didn't I, Campion?' he murmured. 'You certainly pleasured me. So much that I wanted to experience that pleasure again.'

'Now?' Campion quavered, unable to believe that that tiny, husky whisper of sound came from her own throat. What was it about this man that could reduce her to this mass of quivering, desirous flesh?

She wasn't aware of standing up, of moving at all, in fact, but she must have done, because she was in his arms and his hands were going under her sweater to find her breasts. She moaned as he touched them, her nipples instantly responsive.

He undressed her quickly, almost desperately, stripping off his own clothes with swift economy of movement. They made love in front of the fire.

Guy's mouth touched her everywhere, teaching her new things about her sexuality, arousing her to the point where she knew nothing other than her overwhelming need for him.

She reached out to touch him in turn, but he stopped her gently, and as he moved over her in the firelight she realised the reason for his visit to the village.

He saw her glance and said quietly, 'It seemed safest. I didn't think you'd be . . . protected in any way.'

'No. No, I'm not.'

She ought to have felt relieved and pleased, and she did, of course, but a tiny part of her registered the fact that he didn't want there to be any risk of her conceiving his child, and therefore that he didn't want their relationship to be anything other than transitory.

She had expected that this time the intensity of his possession would have lessened, but it was just as fierce, just as tumultuous.

As she lay awake in the aftermath of their lovemaking, she prayed that, when the time came, she would be able to let him go with grace and dignity, and that she would never embarrass him and humiliate herself by revealing how much she loved him.

CHAPTER SEVEN

CAMPION woke up briefly when Guy carried her to bed.

'Can I stay with you, or would you prefer to sleep alone?'

'Stay.'

She said the word drowsily, smiling as she felt the soft brush of his mouth against her skin. She liked the warmth of having him in bed beside her, the sensation of his arm resting over her body, his hand cupping her breast, his legs enmeshed with her own. This was real intimacy—but it would not be hers for ever, she reminded herself.

She woke up early, feeling gloriously, singingly alive. Guy was still asleep, and she crept out of bed and went downstairs to the study.

Barely six o'clock, it was still dark outside, but she had woken up itching to work, and not even the chill of the unheated study could stop her.

The words flowed, unrolling in vivid, quicksilver imagery in her mind. It had been a long time since she had been so captivated by her work; a long, long time, she realised with hindsight, since she had taken such a keen pleasure in what she was doing, since she had felt this sureness that her characters were real and alive.

Lynsey, with her dark curls and quick temper, her pride and her stubborn belief that only she had the right to direct her life; and Dickon, subtle, clever, enigmatic Dickon, who masked his real feelings with his cool courtier's smile.

She had to stop when her wrists began to ache, and was shocked to discover that it was gone eight.

This morning, she *would* make the breakfast and, what was more, this time, she wouldn't ruin the eggs, but first . . .

When she went upstairs, Guy was still asleep. She smiled as she ran her fingertips along her unshaven jaw, feeling the rasp of stubble against her skin. She bent her head and kissed the tip of his nose, and then, giving in to an irresistible impulse, she traced the shape of his mouth with her fingertip. Such a very tender, caring, compassionate mouth. Like the man himself.

Absorbed in her thoughts, she didn't notice his eyes open until Guy murmured, 'Mmm . . . nice.' He bit teasingly at her finger, capturing her wrist and turning his mouth into her open palm.

She shuddered at the sensation that rioted through her, and then closed her eyes as he proceeded to lick delicately at her fingers. He found the pulse beating frantically inside her wrist and stroked it. A thousand wild jolts of pleasure burst through her, making her cry out softly.

This need, this passion, this overwhelming upsurge of sensuality—why had she never known them before?

Because she had never known Guy, she told herself unsteadily.

He was gradually eroding the years of loneliness and mistrust; the doubts and the fears whose seeds Craig had planted within her.

'Guy, let me go,' she protested huskily. 'I was just going to make breakfast.'

'I don't want breakfast. I want you,' he told her

lazily, and then he started to suck slowly on her fingers, and her resistance dissolved in a haze of blissful need.

'Why do you keep on wearing so many clothes?' The words were muffled against her skin as his fingers burrowed beneath her sweater and shirt to find her breasts.

Her breath caught in her throat. In his eyes, she could see the same need she knew he could see in hers.

She was trembling when he finished undressing her. His skin was warm from the bed, and she inhaled the scent of it freedily, biting teasingly at it until he stopped her by taking possession of her mouth with his own.

They made love quickly, fiercely, as though for both of them their time together was precious and threatened.

Afterwards, lying dazed and satiated in his arms, euphoria prompted Campion to ask unsteadily, 'Is it always like this?'

Guy turned to look at her.

'Only with you.'

He was lying; he had to be. Flattering her because it was his natural instinct not to hurt. She had learned that much about him already, but even so she couldn't help treasuring the words, hugging them to her, wondering if he knew how precious they were to a woman who had passed most of her adult life thinking herself sexually deficient. And now here was this man, this very special, wonderful man, telling her that she was wrong, that the pleasure they shared was unique and rare.

She could have loved him for that alone, she admitted later, watching him as they ate their breakfast.

But she had loved him before she had really known him; she had loved him when she had been able to expect nothing from him but contempt and disinterest.

And now?

Now her love had strengthened, grown, and already her mental vow to herself never to tell him how she felt was proving hard to keep.

She *wanted* to tell him; she wanted to exult in her new-found knowledge about herself, but she knew it would be wrong of her to give him that burden.

She was not a fool; she was not the first woman in Guy's life, and she would not be the last. She must accept that what they shared was transitory, and not shadow the present with her fears for the future—a future she would have to live without Guy.

'You're frowning. What's wrong?' Guy put down his coffee-cup abruptly, and caught her pale face in his hand, turning it so that she had to meet his eyes.

'I . . . I was just thinking about my book.'

She moistened her lips as he continued to regard her with that same steady look. She suspected that he knew she was fibbing, but he didn't press her. However, a tiny shadow remained at the back of his eyes and, when he released her, she felt as though she had disappointed him in some way.

After breakfast, she went back to work.

Guy seemed to know instinctively when to and when not to interrupt her. He let her work until lunch time, and then insisted that she leave the typewriter, even though she protested that she wanted to carry on.

'You've done enough. If you don't rest, you'll exhaust yourself.'

Irritation at being dragged away from her work made her snappy.

'What's wrong?' she demanded. 'Don't you trust me? I suppose you want to check what I've done to make sure it's "sexy" enough, before I do any more.'

She knew that taunt was unjustified, even as she said it, but she was not prepared for Guy's reaction.

Instead of retaliating, he simply said quietly, 'We'll discuss it after lunch.'

She wanted to tell him that she didn't want any lunch, but somehow or other she found herself sitting down and eating, and it was only as she did so that she realised how tense she had been. Now, with the tension seeping out of her, she regretted her earlier outburst, and said so, feeling slightly shame-faced.

'Don't apologise. The very fact that you're so absorbed in the book tells me all I need to know about how it's going. Do you know the thing that worried me most of all about it before?'

She shook her head, pouring them both a cup of coffee.

'It was the fact that you were so detached from your characters, especially Lynsey. It was almost as though you felt—I don't know—distaste for her.'

Distaste. Campion frowned, and tried to judge her original manuscript honestly. Not distaste, but dislike, perhaps . . . resentment because, in Lynsey, she had created a woman such as she could never be herself.

'When it came to the historical background, the factual reporting, they were all so good that I knew there had to be a way to make your actual characters come alive to match the rest of your work, and I promised myself that I'd find that way.'

Later, those words were to haunt her, but when she heard them they rang no warning bells.

'How do you think you'll feel about being a successful commercial author?'

'Successful as in "best-selling"?' Campion teased back.

'Oh, definitely.'

'I'm not sure . . .'

'Well, if I were you, I'd start thinking about it, because from what I've read of the rewrites, this book *is* going to be successful.'

She ought to have felt elated, but instead all she did feel was a deep awareness of inner despair because Guy had mentioned the future, but only in abstract terms; he had said nothing to her to hint that he felt that they would be sharing that future.

They were only here for another two weeks, and then she was due to start on her small tour. After that, it was Christmas.

Christmas . . .

'How about going out for a drive this afternoon?' Guy suggested. 'Pembroke is a particularly historic area . . .'

A historic area it might well be, but it was also a cold, wet November afternoon, with mist hanging low over the landscape, and rain dripping miserably from the bare branches of the scrubby trees that grew on the sites of the once powerful castles, whose remains Guy insisted she should see.

Even so, it was possible to imagine what they must have been, and it was most probably the weather that caused her to leave them with an awareness of melancholy and pain.

They stopped in Haverfordwest to buy food, and Guy insisted on dragging her into a local bookshop, where they found two copies of her last book.

They bought paperbacks and magazines, and Guy even insisted on buying a complicated and enormous jigsaw puzzle.

'We always used to get one of these for Christmas,' he told her when she teased him about it in the car on the way back. 'I suppose Ma thought it was a good way of keeping us occupied during the school holidays. She always seemed to choose one with lots of trees, reflected in water . . .'

'Yes, I know the kind you mean.'

'The twins used to lose patience with them.'

Campion glanced at him, and saw the way his face softened.

'What about you?'

'I often felt like giving up, but something always made me keep on until it was finished. Pride, I suppose. I've never liked admitting defeat.'

Why did she had the feeling that she had just been given a warning? A warning about what? Had she been younger, less intelligent, had Guy been a different type of man, she supposed she might have wondered if he had deliberately set out to seduce her because she represented some sort of challenge, but Guy wasn't that type of man; he did not possess that particular shallowness of nature. They were lovers, and if anything she was grateful to him for breaking down her barriers and showing her how very much of a woman she actually was.

While he had been buying some wine, she had noticed a small shop tucked away almost out of sight, and she had gone into it on impulse.

Her purchases were tucked away underneath the books they had bought, and she was still not sure what had prompted her to make them, or how Guy would react.

'Tonight we're going to celebrate,' Guy told her. 'This time, I've bought champagne.'

—They had also bought fresh salmon and other luxuries, Guy insisting he would how Campion how to cook them.

It was dark when they got back, the cottage lights glimmering welcomingly as they turned into the yard.

It took Campion several minutes to analyse the sensation inside her as she got out of the car and, when she did, tears shimmered in her eyes.

What she had experienced was a sense of coming home, of being in a place that was special, of being with *someone* who was special, she recognised, as Guy placed his arm round her shoulder and they walked together to the door.

Unlike her father, Guy was a very physically affectionate man, a man whose compassion and caring in no way detracted from his intense maleness, but rather added an extra dimension to it. She felt safe with him, Campion realised; safe, cherished and protected.

Perhaps it was silly of her to feel those things; after all, she was a modern woman: self-supporting, capable and intelligent, who did not need to look for security of any kind in a man.

Perhaps some instincts could never be entirely lost, she mused as she walked into the kitchen; a woman's dependence on a man went back to those first cave-dwellers, where woman was, by virtue of her ability to bear children, unable to hunt and fend for herself as freely as a man.

She was so deep in thought that Guy had to speak to her twice before she realised what he had said.

'The book again?' he asked.

'Sort of . . .' It was true that her thoughts had led her on to wonder how Lynsey would have dealt with this ancient instinct that still ran so strongly beneath the surface of the female psyche.

'I see. So you're going to desert me again, are you?'

He was only teasing her, but Campion didn't like the need she could feel within herself to please him, and so she reacted defensively, her body tautening slightly as she said, 'That was what I came here for—to work, and I seem to remember that you were the one . . .'

Guy put down the parcels he was carrying and came over to her, taking hold of her hands, and keeping them loosely within the grasp of his own.

'Hey, hold on, I was only teasing! Of course you must work, if that's what you want to do. As a matter of fact, it would give me an opportunity to do a little work of my own.'

He picked up the carrier containing the paperbacks they had bought, and fished out a handful.

These were the ones he had chosen, and Campion saw now that they were all by the same author.

'He's thinking of changing agent, and it may be that he'll come to us. His style isn't quite up to our standard, but that may be the fault of his present publishers. We shall have to see. I don't want to stop you from working, Campion, I just want to make sure that you don't overdo things. You go at things almost obsessively, you know. When you work, you don't eat, you don't relax . . .'

Obsessive—was that how he saw her? She shivered slightly. Was he trying subtly to warn her that she mustn't direct that driving obsession into their relationship? If so, there was no need; she already

knew the truth. After all, he had made her no
promises, no vows, no whispers of love, even in their
most passionate moments . . .

He was putting the books back into the bag and
suddenly he frowned, 'What's this?'

'It's nothing,' she told him hurriedly, reaching out
to snatch it from him. 'Just something I bought.'

Guy looked at her for a moment, plainly aware of
her agitation, and then he handed the carrier to her
with a small smile. She reached for it, but in her
tension let it slide from her grasp. As it fell towards
the floor, Guy caught hold of it, but its tissue-
wrapped contents were already revealed as they
tumbled out of the package.

All her old uncertainties, her fears and her
inadequacies swept back as Campion stood, unable
to move, unable to look away from the delicate satin
garments the tissue paper had revealed. Her face still
burned hot with mortification. If only Guy would say
something, instead of just looking at her in that
steady way.

It seemed an aeon of time before he did.

'Come with me,' he told her quietly, and then,
taking her hand, he drew her upstairs to the room
they shared.

As he had done once before, he stood her in front
of the pier-glass, and then, while she tried not to
tremble, he slowly unfastened the buttons of her
blouse and then peeled it from her skin. Her skirt
followed, and then her underwear, until she was
naked, shivering slightly, more from tension than
cold.

'These——' His hands touched her breasts lightly,
and then moved down over her body. '—you, are so
beautiful, so perfect, that you need no adornment,

no gilding for me to take pleasure in the sight of
you, but, manlike, I can't help the way I feel,
knowing that you wanted to add to such perfection
for my benefit.

'Nothing could feel better than the silk of your
skin; nothing could be more sensuous than the way
your body responds to my touch.' He turned her to
face him and said with a wry smile, 'What did you
think I was going to say?'

She was really shaking now, as she clutched the
underwear to her. It had been an impulse buy, a
desperate yearning to celebrate her new sensuality,
and yet the moment she was out of the shop she
had experienced fear, panic almost, and she had
already decided that the underwear would remain
unworn. To another woman, there might be
nothing provocative about it; it was perfectly
decent and very respectable pure satin underwear,
designed for a woman who liked to feel as feminine
under her clothes as she did outwardly, but it was
so different from the utilitarian underwear she
ordinarily wore that she felt self-conscious and
awkward.

'I . . . I thought you might . . . laugh at me . . .'

She had made him angry. She could sense that in
the very quality of his silence. His body was taut,
as tense as her own, but in a different way.

'Campion, Campion, you *still* don't trust me, do
you?' he said harshly. 'Part of you still thinks I'm
going to turn into another Craig, doesn't it?'

What could she say? Because, in a way, it was
true, only it was not that she didn't trust him. More
that she didn't trust *herself*. Their relationship was
still so new to her, the reality of him actually
wanting her so . . . so almost unbelievable, that she

was afraid to take anything for granted. She was like a child, given a much-longed-for gift and terrified that it might be snatched away from her again, she recognised wryly.

'Surely you know by now that I want you. *You,*' he emphasised fiercely. 'You, whether you come dressed in cotton, or silk and lace.'

'But you prefer me to wear my hair down,' she reminded him.

'For purely selfish reasons. I love the way it feels when I touch it, and when it's all screwed up I can't do that. Trust me, Campion,' he urged her. 'Trust me not to be like Craig. I can't obliterate the past, but I'm not part of it. This is the present.'

He released her slowly.

'Right now, there's nothing I want more than to take you to bed and show you how I feel about you, but that isn't the answer, and making love shouldn't be used in that way. I want you to give me your trust freely . . . when your mind's clear. I'll go down and start dinner.'

Campion dressed in a daze, and it was only when she got downstairs that she realised that she was wearing her new underwear. When she moved, she was conscious of the brush of the satin against her skin. It was a pleasurable sensation, not unlike . . . not unlike the touch of Guy's hands, she admitted self-consciously.

The days passed. Her book grew; it had been almost entirely rewritten, so great had become her absorption in the development of Lynsey's feelings for her husband.

Guy helped her enormously: reading, approving, sometimes pointing out areas of improvement.

She had put on weight, just a few pounds, enough to soften the angularity of her body. When she looked at herself in the mirror, she saw a different Campion, a Campion whose face and body reflected the way she felt. She moved with a new confidence, her body now something in which she took pleasure.

She had even learned to laugh a little at herself, something which was a totally new experience.

She had expected as their time together grew that Guy's desire for her would mellow, but instead it seemed to grow more intense.

Although he was always careful not to hurt her, sometimes when he made love to her she felt as though he was reaching for something he felt was beyond his grasp. Secretly, she began to worry that she was not satisfying him, that there was something lacking in her that caused the ferocity of his passion. And she was too insecure to discuss it with him.

Sometimes she would see him looking at her as though he was waiting for something. Sometimes when they made love and he made her cry out with joy and need she felt as though he was waiting for more, but what more could there be?

Not once had he mentioned seeing her when they returned to London; and so, as their last week together sped by, she found she was slowly distancing herself from him, preparing herself for the time when he would no longer be part of her life.

They still made love; but emotionally she was once again erecting her barriers.

If he sensed it, he said nothing. If he did sense it, he could only be relieved that she was behaving in such an adult manner, she decided. After all, he was the man; if he wanted to put their relationship on a more serious footing, he only had to say. It must be painfully obvious how she felt about him.

The night before they left they were going out for dinner to a small restaurant outside Haverfordwest.

Personally, Campion would rather they had stayed at the cottage, but she suspected that Guy was afraid that if they did she might become too emotional, and that this was his way of making sure that did not happen.

The restaurant was popular and busy. Campion had bought herself a new dress, surprised to find a very expensive boutique in Haverfordwest that stocked designer clothes.

The dress was silk jersey, fluid swathes of fabric that moulded her body discreetly, in a pattern designed to suggest snakeskin.

With it, she wore high-heeled shoes and sheer silk stockings, and even with her heels she was still shorter than Guy.

Since she did not have a coat with her suitable for wearing over it, she was glad that Guy was able to park right outside.

They were offered drinks at the bar; Guy ordered champagne cocktails, but she only sipped at hers. She was wrought-up and tense, wishing with all her heart that she and Guy were alone. This was not how she wanted to celebrate their las night together.

Their last night. Guy looked at her and she trembled. He started to speak, but was interrupted by the waiter informing them that their table was ready.

As they walked to it, Campion was surprised to be the recipient of several admiring male glances. Men looking at *her* . . .

She did not realise that the lustre to her skin, the

confidence in her walk, the air she now carried of being a desirable and desired woman were just as obvious as her old inferiorities had once been.

When they sat down, Guy was frowning. He looked angry about something and Campion felt her heart flutter. This whole evening was a mistake, and now Guy was annoyed.

She reached across the table and touched his hand, her eyes anxious and concerned.

'Guy, what is it? What's wrong?'

He threw down his napkin and said harshly, 'Let's get out of here.'

And, before Campion could object, they were outside in the car park, and Guy was bundling her into the car.

Neither of them spoke on the drive back, Campion because she was half afraid to, in case something she said sparked off the anger she could sense from Guy's tension, and Guy because he seemed to be engrossed in his driving, and whatever it was that had led him to leave the restaurant so precipitously.

Not until they were inside the kitchen did Campion speak. They were leaving first thing in the morning, and so she and Guy had spent the afternoon making sure that they were leaving everything spick and span.

'I suppose I'd better make us something to eat,' she suggested, mentally reviewing the contents of the fridge. They had thrown everything out other than bacon, eggs and bread for their breakfast.

'I don't want anything to eat,' Guy told her tersely.

It was so unlike him to be like this. He was one of the most even-tempered people she had ever

met, capable of anger, it was true, but also capable
of controlling it, of allowing himself to see the
justice of someone else's point of view.

Impulsively she reached out to touch him, and
asked, as she had done in the restaurant, 'Guy,
what is it? What——'

'What is it? It's *this,* damn you! he told her
violently, dragging her into his arms and taking her
mouth fiercely, the pressure of his kiss bruising her
lips, hurting almost. She must have made a sound
of protest, because suddenly he released her,
cupping her face with both his hands and resting
his hot forehead against hers.

'God, I'm sorry . . .'

She only just heard his muffled apology. 'I
wanted to take you out . . . to end . . .' He shook
his head, and when he spoke again his voice was
raw and husky, 'But all I could think of was how
much I wanted to make love to you, and how much
I hated not being able to touch you.'

Campion shivered, so closely did his words
match her own feelings.

'I was so damn jealous. All those other men
looking at you. God, you're making me react like a
Victorian . . .'

Guy, jealous? It made her heart melt with
tenderness and love. She turned her head and
kissed him, feeling the hard smoothness of his jaw
against her lips. She touched his throat with her
tongue-tip and felt him swallow, his hands
tightening on her arms. She unfastened the buttons
of his shirt, slowly dragging her open mouth
against his skin, thrilling to the increased thud of
his heart and the rapid harshness of his breathing.

They made love as they had done once before, in

front of the sitting-room fire, Campion uncaring that her new dress lay in a crumpled heap where Guy had thrown it.

It was late when they went to bed, as though neither of them wanted to waste a single second of their time together, but Guy had still said nothing about seeing her in London, about needing her inhis life . . . about wanting her.

He had talked about her forthcoming tour, he had asked her what she intended doing over Christmas, but he had made no suggestion that they spend any time together. This silence, so curiously at odds with the intensity of his love-making, saddened her, but she had to accept it. Guy was as he was. He had given her joy and pleasure; he had given her back her belief in herself; it would be sheer greed to ask for anything more.

She woke up early, tense and aching, still caught up in a dream where she had seen Guy walk away from her. She reached for him, wanting the comfort of his nearness, touching his skin with obsessive fierce need.

He woke up, murmuring soft, approving noises of pleasure at her touch. His hand stroked her breast, finding the already erect nipple. His mouth caressed her skin, and she shuddered in pleasure as she felt the light grate of his teeth against the sensitive crest.

Her body pulsed with need to be filled by him. The aroused strength of him pressing against her increased that need, and she moved against him erotically. She knew now those things that gave him the most pleasure but, when she reached out instinctively to caress him, he stopped her.

'No. No, we can't . . .' His mouth left her breast to mutter harshly in her ear, 'You won't be protected. I could make you pregnant.'

Make her pregnant. Betrayingly, her body thrilled at the prospect. Guy's child. She could almost feel the spasm of pleasure contracting her womb at the thought of conceiving his child.

Madness! she told herself. What she was contemplating was madness—folly—crass self-indulgence, but she touched him again, and felt the shudder that jarred his body as he tried to control his need.

He moved and she moved with him, possessed by an earthly, feminine power that overwhelmed all his protests, gently seducing him to the point where he cried out his great need to her and entered her fiercely, each thrust of his body within hers heightening both her pleasure and her instinctive awareness that this would be the last time they shared this very special intimacy.

It was over too quickly, leaving her both drained and replete. Guy lay on his back at her side, breathing heavily, making no move to touch her.

CHAPTER EIGHT

CORNWALL in December. Not the best time to visit this part of the world, Campion reflected grimly—not for the first time—as she stared out of her hotel bedroom window.

Almost a week since they had left Wales, and not a word from Guy. But what had she expected? That he would somehow discover in her absence that he couldn't live without her? Hardly. She had been a temporary obsession, like one of the jigsaw puzzles he had felt compelled to solve; once the picture lay clear before him, he could go back to his normal way of life. She closed her eyes in anguish, remembering. To Guy, she had represented a challenge, that was all. He had meant to make sure she finished her book, and if making her fall in love with him was what it took . . . Well, he was a professional, and he had certainly managed to make her inject some real emotion into the story.

That last day they had had together, he had deliberately talked about *her* future in terms that made it clear he intended to play no part in it, mentioning her forthcoming tour, but sidestepping any mention of Christmas, giving her no indication of where he would be or how he would be spending his time. There had been no mention of him seeing her again. In fact, his conversation with her about this tour had been purely practical: questions about where she would be staying and for how long, and in which shops her signing sessions were being undertaken. Questions, surely, that any concerned agent mught ask an author, but hardly those of a lover.

In fact, the only person who had seemed concerned about her was Lucy, who had been in touch to confirm their Christmas arrangement before the tour started. Campion had promised to arrive early, so that she could help her friend prepare for the onslaught of expected guests.

Campion shivered. Lucy had noticed the change in her immediately, commenting on her unconfined hair and searching her face closely. 'It must be a man,' she had said at last. 'Do I know him?'

'No,' Campion lied, not denying the first charge.

'Am I going to?' Lucy asked in a more gentle voice.

Campion knew what she was really saying. She managed a wry smile, hoping it successfully masked her inner pain. 'No, I'm afraid not,' she said as lightly as she could. 'It wasn't that sort of relationship.'

'Married?' Lucy guessed, plainly rather disconcerted.

'No.' Campion drew a deep breath. 'I decided I'd let Craig spoil enough of my life. The—the man I was with—made me realise that I'd been alone too long, that's all.'

It sounded plausible enough, and perhaps her tone warned Lucy not to press any harder. Lucy smiled and said lightly, 'Well, whoever he is, he's certainly transformed you. I'm going to have to keep an eye on Howard while you're around from now on, that's for sure.'

Yes, Guy had transformed her, inwardly as well as outwardly. Campion levered herself away from the window. This tour was giving her too much time to

think, to remember. She was reduced to poring over
the past, looking for significant details that she'd
missed in the joy of Guy's company. And suddenly
the memory of Craig, whose very existence she had
forgotten until she needed an excuse to give Lucy,
began to nag like a toothache. Craig had come from
a poor family, just like Guy, and had got rid of all
the traces of his past. He had seemed charming,
attentive, caring . . . just like Guy. And Craig had
never seen her as a person, only as a means to an end.
If he hadn't wanted something Campion could give
him, he would never have come near her. Craig
hadn't got what he wanted, but it was beginning to
look as though Guy had.

She would be better off working, she thought with
sudden savagery, turning her talent of invention into
a new book. Guy had promised to let her know what
the publishers thought of her changed manuscript,
but as yet she had heard nothing. He would have to
contact her at some point, she thought wryly, or else
she would be looking for a new agent.

All she could do was to try to live each day at a
time, and to hope that somehow the pain would ease.
Already she had lost the weight she had gained;
already her face had a fragile quality of vulnerability
about it, a yearning, lost loneliness that people saw
and wondered about, but dared not question for fear
of trespassing.

Tonight, she was having dinner with the owner of
a local bookshop; tomorrow, there was a radio interview and a signing session. Once, the publicity might
have unnerved her—now it was a way of filling in
time before she heard from Guy French.

She looked at the dress she had hung up, ready to
wear. It was the dress she had brought for Guy, the

dress she had worn on their last night together . . . A
quiver of emotion darted through her, and she
fought to keep it at bay. She had known there would
be pain, but she had never imagined it could be like
this. When Craig had left her she had been hurt, but
much of it, she now recognised, had been shock and
the spiteful destruction of her self-confidence . . .
Craig's retaliation for not getting his way. But this
pain was different in quality. So intense, so overwhelming, that nothing else mattered . . . nothing.

It amazed Campion that she could feel so
unhappy, and yet at the same time look so—so
blooming. Her skin glowed, her hair shone, and she
couldn't help but be aware of the interested and
approving looks that men now gave her.

She had Guy to thank for that, for the almost
visible patina of womanliness that now clung so
alluringly to her. She hadn't gone back to wearing
her hair up; instead, she had had it trimmed to
accentuate its thick curl, and she had even started
experimenting cautiously with make-up. She used
some now, wondering what it was that Antony
Polroon, the bookshop owner, wanted to discuss
with her.

He was a thin, dark man in his mid-thirties, wiry
and slightly intense, and very Cornish.

Normally, he was the kind of man she would have
avoided on sight, but her new-found confidence had
helped her to see him as a fellow human being, and
not another man who was bound to condemn her as
unworthy of his attention.

They were dining at the hotel. Campion arrived
downstairs several minutes late and found him
waiting there for her.

His admiring glance told her that he approved of

her dress, and she tried desperately not to remember another man's attention focusing on it, another man removing it from her body and caressing her until . . .

She realised that Antony was watching her curiously.

'I'm sorry . . . This tour has been something of a strain, and I'm beginning to feel it. What was it you just said?'

'Nothing important. Only that you're a very beautiful woman,' he told her wryly.

A very beautiful woman. Two men had told her that now. Funny how meaningless the words were. She didn't want compliments, adulation, attention; she wanted Guy. She wanted his presence at her side, his smile, his warmth in bed, she wanted his love.

'Shall we go into dinner?' Antony suggested.

He was an entertaining companion and, in other circumstances, Campion would probably have enjoyed the evening. As it was . . .

As it was the ache of missing Guy had become a physical pain inside her, a pain so intense, in fact, that half-way through the main course she had to excuse herself and rush to the ladies' cloakroom.

When she came back, looking slightly green and very apologetic, Antony got to his feet.

'I'm sorry. Will you excuse me? I must have picked up a bug of some kind. I'm afraid we're going to have to call it a day.'

'I'll see you to your room.'

Campion demurred, but Antony insisted and, if she was honest, she was feeling slightly dizzy, as well as very queasy.

Too many hours spent travelling, too many new faces, or simply too much heartache over Guy.

Riding in the lift increased her feeling of nausea,

and she was glad to lean on Antony when it rocked
to a standstill and he helped her out. She had never
fainted in her life, but now she was desperately
afraid that she was about to do so.

Her room wasn't very far from the lift, and she
nodded weakly when Anthony asked if she had her
key.

'It's here in my bag,' she told him, passing the
small evening purse over to him. While he opened
it and removed the key, she leaned weakly against
the wall.

She felt terrible, even worse than she had done
one year when she had had 'flu.

She heard the sound of the lift doors closing; it
seemed to fill her head like a dull roar.

Antony opened the door of her room and held it
open with his foot while he supported the sagging
weight of her body in his arms.

'Would you like me to find a doctor?'

Even to take those few steps that would get her
inside her room was an appalling effort. She shook
her head, unable to speak. Several yards away
from them, down the corridor, the lift door
opened.

'I'll be all right in a few minutes . . .' All she
wanted was to be left alone. She felt terrible, but if
she said as much she suspected that Antony would
insist on informing the hotel, and then they would
fuss, when all that was really wrong with her was
that she was missing Guy. *Missing* him? She almost
laughed aloud. Without him, her life was an empty
desert, a wasteland, a landscape scoured and
ravished and left for dead.

'Come on. You should be in bed.'

As Antony helped her inside, she was dimly

conscious of a man walking down the corridor.

'That's odd,' Antony commented as he closed the door behind them. 'He must have got the wrong floor or something. He got as far as your door and then he turned back. Looked furious about something as well.'

Campion's head was pounding, her mouth felt dry and sour, and the last thing she was interested in was her fellow guests.

'Are you sure you'll be all right?' Antony pressed. 'You . . .'

'I'll be fine. I'm sorry I spoiled our evening.'

'I'll ring you in the morning.' Antony walked back to the door and opened it.

In the morning she was leaving for Falmouth, but Campion didn't have the energy to tell him so. She heard the door click locked as he left, and she didn't even have the strength to get undressed, but instead fell asleep as she was.

She woke up in the early hours, stiff and cold, her muscles cramped. She undressed and had a bath before crawling into bed. She could never remember feeling so exhausted. Her stomach felt hollow and empty, and she tried to remember when she had last eaten before last night.

She was appalled to discover that her last proper meal had been the breakfast she had shared with Guy. She had only picked at food since then. No wonder she was feeling ill.

She was woken by the alarm call she had booked, and got up feeling lethargic and drained. She ordered a room-service breakfast, but when it arrived she could only pick at it, her stomach rebelling at the sight of food. She packed her case and rang down for a porter, and then went down stairs to meet the publishers' agent who was accompanying her on the tour, as previously arranged.

Kyla Harris was a plump, efficient girl in her mid-twenties, with a mass of dark curls and a warm smile.

'Are you all right?' she frowned when she saw Campion's pale face.

'I think I've picked up a bug.'

'Oh dear, and just before Christmas as well.'

Campion realised that Kyla was looking anxiously at her, probably dreading hearing her say that she wanted to cancel the tour, but what was the point? She could be sick just as easily here in Cornwall as she could in London, she told herself sardonically.

'Oh, by the way,' Kyla asked, when their cases were stowed in the back of her car, 'someone was looking for you last night. Did he find you?'

'Someone?' Campion felt her heart leap. 'Who?'

Kyla shrugged. 'I don't know. One of the girls on reception said that someone came in, asking for us. She gave him your room number. Local press, I expect . . .'

'Oh, yes,' Campion agreed dully. 'Press, of course.'

For a moment, she had been stupid enough to hope that her visitor might have been Guy.

If Guy wanted to speak to her, he was hardly likely to come rushing down to Cornwall. He knew where she was. All he had to do was to lift the telephone . . .

In Falmouth, she did a radio interview and then a signing session. By five o'clock in the afternoon she was exhausted. One day left and then back home; and she still had all her Christmas shopping to do.

Lucy and Howard always made a big event of Christmas, with lavish presents, and she always liked to repay their generosity with carefully chosen gifts.

A display in a shop window caught her eye as she and Kyla made their way back to the car, and she stopped to glance at it.

An old-fashioned polished crib was hung with hand-made appliquéd quilts and matching bolsters, some brightly coloured, others delicately pastel.

One in particular caught her eye; she knew that Lucy would love it, but might it not be tempting fate to buy it for her for a Christmas present, especially in view of her past problems?

She could buy it and keep it until the baby was born, she told herself and, asking Kyla to wait, she went inside.

When they reached their hotel, she apologised to Kyla, and asked her if she would mind if she ate in her room.

'No, you go ahead. You look washed out. Are you sure you want to go on?'

'There's only one more day,' Campion reminded her.

One more day, and then it would be a week since she had last heard from Guy. A week. She shivered, huddling deeper into her coat.

The tour was over, successfully, so Kyla said. Somehow or other, Campion had smiled and talked her way through a succession of interviews and chat shows. Somehow, she had managed to sign books and answer questions, and now at last it was over.

Like her relationship with Guy, she thought, as

Kyla saw her safely on to the London train.

Her bloom had gone; it had been a brief flowering indeed, before shrivelling in the forest of loneliness and pain. Lynsey's story had carried her away into fantasy, making her believe that she could be what she was not—a woman for loving. Now she had to face the rest of her life without Guy, because she couldn't bear to hear the words of rejection on his lips, as they had once been on Craig's rejection had crippled her; Guy's, she knew, could kill her. Better to go back to the old, cold life and never see him again. Try to ride out the hurt. Perhaps one day she'd be able to put it into a book, she thought hollowly.

The journey seemed to take forever. London was cold and wet, and when she let herself into her flat all she wanted to do was to fall into bed.

The phone woke her, and for one crazy moment she thought it must be Guy. She picked up the receiver, her hand shaking.

'Campion, are you all right?'

The incisive tones of her agent's voice made her heart drop.

'Helena, I'm fine,' she lied. 'What about you?'

'Oh, I've been giving the all clear now, and I'm raring to get back to work. In fact, I *am* back. That's why I'm ringing you. How did the tour go?

'Quite well.'

There was a small silence, as though something in her colourless tone had reached the other woman.

'Well, I've got some good news for you. The publishers are thrilled with your last manuscript. Guy's left me a note saying that they want to get it into production as quickly as possible . . . Campion, are you there?'

She was gripping the receiver so hard, her bones hurt.

'Yes . . . yes . . . I am. Guy's away, then, is he?'

Oh, God, what was she doing to herself? If he wanted her to know his movements, he would have told her himself. Was this what love did to you, reducing you to begging for scraps of information, destroying all your pride and integrity?

'Yes. He hasn't had a proper break this year, and he suddenly decided that he wanted to get away. He's gone to visit his sister, apparently. Look, when can we meet? The publishers are keen for you to do something else for them. A family saga this time, perhaps—historical again, of course——'

She had wronged Guy, Campion thought numbly. His absence was nothing so personal as a snub, nothing to do with Craig's kind of petty revenge. She had simply been put back into her proper perspective as a very small part of a successful man's life; a professional challenge that had had some importance for as long as the job lasted, but now just one more name on his agency's list, another writer whose work he had an interest in selling.

Work . . . the universal panacea. Campion closed her eyes.

'I seem to have picked up some sort of bug, Helena. Can we leave it until after Christmas?'

She could tell from the small silence that Helena was surprised, and no wonder. In the past, she had allowed nothing to interfere with her work.

'Well, yes, of course. You'll be spending Christmas with Lucy and Howard as usual, I expect?'

'Yes.'

'Well, I had hoped to tempt you out to a celebratory lunch . . .'

A celebratory lunch. Campion's stomach heaved, and she felt guilty at her lack of enthusiasm.

'I'd love to,' she lied, 'but this tour has left me rather behind. I'll have a think about another book over Christmas and get in touch with you after the New Year,' she added as a conciliatory gesture.

When she hung up, she sat and hugged her arms around herself, as though by so doing she could contain the fiery spread of her pain.

Surely Guy could have given the good news himself? Or was this his way of underlining the fact that their relationship was over, that she was now in his past and that that was where he wanted her to stay? Was that how these things were done? He wasn't an unkind man, far from it, and she did not have the experience to judge how a man was likely to react when he wanted to end an emotional involvement.

Emotional? For her, perhaps, but for him?

Don't think about it. Don't brood, she chastened herself. All she really wanted to do was to pull the bedcovers round her body and lie there and mourn, but she couldn't do that. She had to find a way of going on with her life without him, of finding a purpose—a reason for going on.

In the meantime, she had promised Lucy her help, and she had also virtually promised Helena a new book.

She dialled the number of Lucy's London home. Her housekeeper answered and then put her through to Lucy.

'This is ridiculous! Neither Mrs Timmins nor Howard will let me lift a finger. I keep telling them that pregnancy is a perfectly natural state. How did the tour go?'

'Fine. Do you still want my help with your Christmas preparations?'

'Yes, please. I've had the most wonderful idea for the drawing-room. I think this year we'll go all traditional. Real fir branches, a huge tree, Victorian decorations . . .'

Campion did her best to sound enthusiastic.

Lucy wanted to leave for Dorset on Tuesday, she told her, and before then she had heaps of shopping to do.

'Howard is insisting that I take Paul and the Rolls wherever I go. Isn't it ridiculous? He won't so much as let me carry one parcel,' she complained.

They agreed to meet mid-morning. She found she tried easily, Lucy told her, and often had to have a rest in the afternoon.

'And you should see me! I'm huge . . . enormous . . . and only four months . . .'

As she hung up, Campion found that her eyes were stinging with tears. Lucy was so lucky. A husband she loved, his child to look forward to . . .

Stop feeling so sorry for yourself, she derided. Compared with millions of women, she was lucky. Maybe, but she didn't feel it.

Despite her claim that she was taking things easy, Lucy managed to fit in an exhausting amount of shopping. Or was it simply that, because she herself could not get into the spirit of Christmas, *she* found it exhausting? Campion wondered late one afternoon, after Paul, the chauffeur, had dropped her off.

'Heavens!' Lucy had exclaimed in concern when

they finally left Harrods. 'You look ready to drop, and Campion, you're losing far too much weight. Are you sure you're all right?'

All right? Physically, there could be nothing much wrong with her; but emotionally . . . that was a different story.

Somehow or other, she had managed to fit her own shopping in between helping Lucy. She had seen the nursery being planned for the new baby, and had heard all about the one being designed for the Dorset house, and she had listened as attentively as she could, but all the time it was as though her real attention was turned inwards, waiting to hear a voice she suspected she would probably never hear again.

She had to accept it. Guy was *not* going to get in touch with her.

It was over. *Finito*. Finished.

But that didn't stop her from thinking about him, from wondering where he was, what he was doing, who he was with, whether he ever spared a thought for her.

Why should he? His self-imposed task to ensure that she finished her book on time and successfully was over. If he did think about her, it could only be to congratulate himself on having achieved his aim, she thought bitterly. No doubt now all his time and attention was given to another writer's problems.

She remembered how, on first seeing him, she had automatically pictured him in expensive, exclusive surroundings, wining and dining high-powered publishing executives, while he sought the best possible deal for his clients. She had seen him as smooth and sophisticated, as the kind of man it would be impossible to trust. She had seen him as being without depth, all plausible surface charm hiding instincts as rapacious as those of a shark; a man whose loyalty to his writers only went as far as their last successful book; but she had been wrong, as he had proved to her.

But she *wasn't* wrong about his lack of desire to pursue their relationship. Over and over again she had reflected on everything he had said to her, on every nuance of every word. Never once had he mentioned them having a future together, and so perhaps it had been naïve of her to hope that he would want to get in touch with her. Face it, she told herself brutally, you aren't the first woman he's made love to. And yet there had been times when he had touched her when she had felt so sure that he was experiencing exactly the same deep intensity of feeling as she was herself.

Wishful thinking, she told herself acidly. Foolish daydreams that had nothing to do with reality.

Tuesday dawned, icy cold with grey clouds. Snow was forecast, Lucy told her excitedly when she joined her in the car.

A dull inertia possessed Campion, an inability to do anything other than simply be. She felt like an animal wanting desperately to go into hiberation. She felt . . . she felt as though there was no meaning, no purpose in her life any more.

'Tell me about the new book,' Lucy commanded, once Paul had stowed Campion's cases in the boot of the Rolls, with her own parcels. 'I bumped into Helena the other day. She was raving about it. She says it's the best thing you've ever done. And all with Guy French's help, so I understand.'

Campion's mouth went dry. She knew that her very silence was causing Lucy to look at her speculatively, but she wasn't ready to talk about Guy yet, not even to her best friend.

She turned her head away.

'Oh, Campion—it's Guy, isn't it? You're in love with him. I'm sorry.' Lucy's hand touched hers. 'I didn't mean to pry.'

How easily she had betrayed herself. So easily, that surely Guy himself must have known how she felt about him. Maybe that knowledge had contributed towards his decision not to see her again. He didn't want the burden of her emotional hunger for him.

Stop thinking about him, she told herself. It won't do any good.

'I felt the baby move this morning. It was the most wonderful sensation. Howard's like a dog with two tails!'

'Everything's OK, then?' Campion roused herself enough to ask.

'Yes, thank God. I couldn't have borne to lose this baby. The specialist thinks I should be safe now, although he warned me to take things easy . . .' She laughed, a clear, trilling sound that stirred envy in Campion's normally unenvious heart. 'I don't get much opportunity to be anything else. Howard and Mrs Timmins between them have me wrapped in cotton wool.'

Lucy's housekeeper had left for the house ahead of them, and when the Rolls turned in between the stone gate-posts they could see smoke curling from the house's many chimneys, and lights glimmering in the windows.

'Mmm—you know what I'm looking forward to

now? Some of Mrs T's home-made scones, dripping with butter, and a huge, hot fire . . .' groaned Lucy.

Lucy's grandfather had removed all the original fireplaces, bricking them up in the bedrooms, but, although he had installed central heating, Howard had scoured architectural salvage depots for period replacements, and Campion had to admit that it had been worth while.

All the guest rooms had their own fires, and Lucy was fortunate in having a devoted and extremely well-paid staff who kept them cleaned and lit.

It was one of the pleasures of Christmas with Howard and Lucy to go up to one's room and bask in front of the luxury of a real fire. A luxury indeed, when combined with the discreet central heating the house also boasted.

The house had once been the hub of a small country estate. Virtually all the land had been sold off in the past, although Howard had bought back a few fields.

Howard was a traditionalist, and one of the traditions he had revived, and which Campion suspected he thoroughly enjoyed, was playing Father Christmas for the local children at a party which they always gave the Sunday before Christmas.

As Mrs Timmins opened the door to welcome them in, Campion saw that a huge fir tree was already in place in the hall. Clucking and fussing, Mrs Timmins hurried them into the sitting-room. This room was particularly Lucy's own. A half-finished tapestry she enjoyed working on when she stayed at the house stood to one side of the fire.

The colour scheme of soft peaches with touches of blue was essentially feminine and light. Lucy had a gift for décor, Campion acknowledged, admiring the carefully chosen antiques and the bowls of winter greenery which highlighted their soft sheen.

This house, for all its elegance, was very much home, and it was easy to picture children sitting in this room, playing.

'George says we're going to have snow tonight,' Mrs Timmins warned them.

George lived in the village and looked after the gardens; he was also famous for his weather predictions.

'I know, isn't it exciting!'

Mrs Timmins gave Lucy an indulgent look, which changed to a slight frown as Campion took off her coat.

'Why, miss, you *have* lost weight,' she exclaimed disapprovingly. 'What have you been doing with yourself?'

Mrs Timmins, herself a comfortably padded women in her fifties, had strong ideas about diets and what she termed 'faddy eating'.

'Be warned, she'll do her best to feed you up while you're here,' Lucy prophesied when the older woman left the room. 'Actually, she's right, Campion. You are too thin.'

The sympathetic look that accompanied the words told her that her old friend suspected the reason for her rapid weight loss.

'You look tired as well. Would you prefer to go straight up to your room? Howard won't be back in time for dinner, but I was hoping we could get most of the decorating done tomorrow, so that means an early start . . .'

'I *am* tired,' Campion admitted. 'In fact, I feel tired all the time.'

'Well, I can sympathise, that's exactly how I felt the first weeks I was pregnant. I think Howard thought I'd got sleeping sickness!'

Pregnant. Campion stood up jerkily. Oh, God, no! She couldn't be, coud she? Guy had always been so careful. Apart from the first time and the last.

'Campion, are you all right?'

'Fine. I think I will go and lie down, if you don't mind.'

Pregnant. Of coure she couldn't be. Campion lay on the bed, staring up at the pleated silk ceiling of the four-poster. She would know, surely? There would be unmistakable signs.

Like being sick and feeling tired, a traitorous voice whispered.

No, she was panicking over nothing. It was true that her body cycles were normally very reliable, but there had been odd occasions when she had experienced the odd hiccup, the odd missed period, and this time . . . Well, she had put it down to the fact that she was so emotionally upset.

One missed period, a little nausea, oppressive tiredness. What did they add up to, after all?

Nothing . . .

Guy's child.

She closed her eyes and swallowed. That frantic desire she had experienced to conceive his child had been a momentary madness. She was not of the valiant breed of women able to support and rear a child on her own.

Financially, yes, she could do it, but there were

other and, to her mind, more important considerations. She and her child would be completely alone. She had no family, no support network to help her to teach her child the reality of family life, the kind of life she would want her child to have. And she did not have the reserves within herself to be both mother and father. Oh, God, what was she going to do?

Don't panic. You could be wrong.

Could be? She must pray that she *was*. How soon could one tell positively? If she had conceived on that last night . . .

It was pointless doing anything yet. She could wait until after Christmas. Until she was back in London.

Guy's child.

When Lucy looked in on her half an hour later, she found her fully dressed and fast asleep, a small smile curling her mouth.

Lucy sighed and didn't wake her, and then thought guiltily of the telephone call she had just made.

Never interfere in other people's lives was Howard's motto. Lucy would just have to hope that on this occasion he was wrong.

'If you could just move the star a little to the left, Paul. There, how do you think that looks?' Lucy appealed to Campion as they both stood back to admire the tree.

'Wonderful,' Campion told her, and it was true.

Dark, glossy greenery, rich red candles, and the sparkle of crystal candle-holders were reflected in the Venetian mirror above the fireplace.

In the window, the tree gleamed and sparkled,

the red satin bows she and Lucy had spent most of
the afternoon making, shimmering against the
branches. Baubles painted with Victorian scenes
hung on red loops, and the tree lights were tiny darts
of white fire illuminating the whole scene.

'Well, we should just about be ready in time for
the children's party, and then it's Christmas Eve, and
everyone else will be arriving.'

The last thing Campion really wanted was to be
part of a noisy house party, but what was the alter-
native? A Christmas spent alone, moping in her flat,
with Lucy offended because she wasn't joining them.

She refused to allow herself to think about the
cottage; about snow piled high outside the windows,
and a fire burning warmly in the sitting-room grate.
They couldn't have had a tree like this one, of course,
but there could have been a small one; decorated with
old-fashioned candles in case the electricity went off.
They could have hung stockings from the mantel-
piece, and the turkey could have cooked slowly and
succulently in the Rayburn.

It took the prick of salt tears behind her eyelids to
bring her back to reality. What was she doing to
herself? Guy had never once indicated that they
should spent Christmas together, and in her heart of
hearts Campion had not expected him to; he would
have commitments with his own family, she was sure,
but they could perhaps have met, have shared one
day together . . . Stop it! she warned herself fiercely.
All she was doing was adding to her own torment.
The only time she and Guy had discussed Christmas,
she remembered telling him she would be staying
with Lucy, as she had done for the last few years,
explaining to him how far their friendship went back.
However, if he had even indicated that he wanted to

see her, she knew that Lucy would have generously accepted her excuses and encouraged her to be with the man she loved.

But that was only fantasy. Guy did *not* want her.

'Howard, what do you think?' Lucy asked as her husband walked into the room.

Watching them together as he walked over and slid his arm round his wife's waist, Campion was appallingly aware of her own inner pain and loneliness.

'Wonderful,' Howard responded, but he was looking at Lucy and not at the tree.

He bent his head to kiss her, and Lucy gave him a playful push. 'Not in front of Campion! You'll embarrass her.'

'What time are the kids due to arrive?' Howard asked, releasing her reluctantly.

'About three. Campion and I have got all the presents wrapped and named. Your Father Christmas outfit is upstairs waiting for you. By the way, we've got one or two extras this year. Neighbours' children,' she added in an offhand manner, but, oddly, Campion had the impression that for some reason her friend was nervous.

'Time to go and get ready,' she added, smiling at Campion. 'I hope you've brought something child-proof with you.'

Experience of previous Christmas parties meant that she had, and as Campion donned the tartan dress, with its neat, white collar and silky bow, she reflected that it was just as well it was washable, because by the end of the afternoon it would probably be covered in smears from sticky fingers.

The weather forecast had been right, and they had a faint riming of snow, with more promised.

The first batch of children arrived well wrapped up and pink-cheeked.

It was a rule that no presents were handed out until everyone had arrived and, to keep the younger children occupied until they did, Paul had been deputised to organise games.

The doorbell was jut chiming for the umpteenth time when one small boy fell over and started to howl.

'Oh, dear!' Torn between rushing to his aid and opening the door in the absence of Mrs Timmins, who was setting out the tea, Lucy looked helplessly from Campion to the small, sprawled figure on the floor.

'I'll deal with the tears, you deal with the door,' Campion suggested.

Despite her lack of contact with young children, she had always had a surprising affinity with them. She picked up the little boy and carried him through into Lucy's sitting-room, where his howls gradually decreased to muffled sobs and then silence. He was crying, Campion learned, because someone had taken his car.

Promising to restore it to him, Campion dried his eyes and distracted him by asking him what he wanted from Father Christmas.

The list that was enthusiastically delivered was demoralisingly technical. What had happened to train sets and skates? Campion wondered, feeling a stab of sympathy for the parents who were expected to produce this cornucopia.

'Shall we go back and see what everyone else is doing?' she suggested, satisfied that the tears were forgotten.

He wanted to be carried, and she willingly

obliged, opening the door and then coming to an appalled halt.

Across the width of the hall, with his back to hr, talking to Lucy, stood Guy.

Campion's heart leaped like a landed salmon. She could actually feel the physical jerk of it lifting in her body. Her arms tightened round her wriggling burden.

Oh, God, what was *Guy* doing here? Did he know that she was here? She suspected not. Oh, how could Lucy have done this to her? She put the little boy down, intent on escape before Guy turned his head and saw her. She couldn't endure the humiliation of meeting him like this, or knowing that her friend had probably engineered his appearance, without suspecting that she was the very last person he would want to see.

She fled into the kitchen, and from there upstairs, using the stairs that had been used exclusively by the servants.

Two women were standing on the landing. One of them was vaguely familiar, for some reason, the other was elegant and *soignée,* with a cool, languid accent.

'Poor Guy, he really didn't want to come, did he? I wonder why?'

Campion stood transfixed. Neither of the women noticed her standing near the top of the staircase. There was a note of restraint in the brunette's voice as she responded quietly, 'I think he's just tired. He's been very busy at work recently.'

'Oh, yes, I know all about that!' Amused malice almost rippled from the blonde's tongue.

'Hart's were amazed at the changes he managed

to get that Roberts woman to make in her manuscript. Very prim and proper the original work
was, not at all what Adam Hart wanted. I heard
that he was ready to break the contract, but Guy
promised him that he'd find a way to get her to toe
the line. Rumour has it that he spent three weeks
shacked up with her somewhere, helping her with
the alterations.'

Campion felt sick. The acid, knowing way the
blonde woman was taking about her—about the
time she had spent with Guy—made her feel soiled,
used.

'That's just gossip, Sandra,' the brunette said
sharply, 'and I shouldn't repeat it in front of Guy
if I were you.'

'Poor Guy! I don't suppose he *does* want it
known that he had to take the woman to bed to get
her to change her manuscript. What's she like?
Have you met her?' she asked idly.

'No, I haven't—and I think we should go downstairs now.'

The brunette's tone was distinctly unfriendly
now. She walked towards the stairs, and the blonde
followed her, leaving Campion alone and shaking.

What she had heard confirmed every worst fear,
including those she had forced herself to suppress.
Guy had made love to her not because he wanted
her, not because he desired her, even in passing . . .
but because of her book. Oh, God, why hadn't she
followed her own instincts? They had told her
clearly enough that a man like Guy French could
never have found her attractive, but she had chosen
to ignore them. She had chosen to go and make a
fool of herself.

She buried her burning face in her hands. The

thought of people discussing her relationship with Guy the way she had just heard it being discussed made her stomach heave.

She only just made it to her bedroom.

She was re-applying her make-up when Lucy knocked and walked in, looking concerned.

'So you're here.'

'Yes. I wasn't feeling very well. Lucy, would you mind if I don't come down? I . . .' To her chagrin, tears flodded her eyes.

'Campion, what is it?'

Instantly Lucy was at her side, her arms going round her, her face concerned.

'I don't know. I'm just not feeling well. Perhaps I ought to go back to London . . . I don't want to spoil your Christmas.'

'You're not going anywhere, especially if you aren't well. First thing tomorrow, I'm going to get Dr Jamieson to come and have a look at you . . .'

'No. No, that won't be necessary. Perhaps I will come down.'

'I shouldn't have invited Guy, should I?' Luch said quietly, guessing what was wrong. 'His sister Meg is one of our neighbours. She's married to Tait Drummond, so I knew you wouldn't recognise the name, and I thought it might be a good way of getting the two of you together . . .'

Guy's sister . . . the brunette who had looked so familiar!

'I shouldn't have interfered.' Lucy looked upset.

'You meant well. Has he gone?'

'Yes.' Lucy crossed her fingers behing her back. 'Look, if you don't feel well, why don't you go and sit in the library for a while until the kids have gone? I'll get Mrs Timmins to bring you something to eat.'

Campion looked wryly at her. The library was her favourite room in the house, a wonderful, book-lined retreat.

'All right. I'll follow you down.'

Campion was half-way across the hall when she heard him call her name. Lucy had lied to her, after all.

She wanted to run, but how could she, with four dozen children milling around, and their mothers looking on with interested eyes? He touched her arm and her skin burned. She couldn't bear to look at him. Where was the blonde? Where was his sister?

'So you *are* here.'

'Lucy is my friend,' she told him without turning her head. 'I always spend Christmas with them. Remember, I told you?'

'Yes, yes you did, didn't you? You don't look well,' he added abruptly.

'I'm just a little tired. Excuse me, would you? I . . .' She started to move away and winced as his fingers gripped her arm.

'My God, is that all you can say to me? Campion, I . . .'

How could he do this to her? She could have cried out at the agony he was inflicting. Why was he continuing with this farcical display of concern? Of caring? Obviously, he didn't know what she had overheard. Perhaps he was already looking ahead, to her next book. She literally shook with rage and anguish at the thought of his duplicity.

'Please let me go, Guy,' she said, as evenly as she

could.

'I want to talk to you.'

He really was a good actor, she marvelled. He sounded almost distraught, even a little frantic, and the look in his eyes . . . If she hadn't known better, she could almost have mistaken it for an anguish to match her own.

'What about?' she asked politely, and as distantly as she might a stranger. 'I really must go, Guy. I promised Lucy I'd help her with the food.'

'I take it you're not here alone?'

Not here alone? There was an odd glitter in his eyes. His mouth was tight and hard.

'That's right. I'm not,' she lied, hating him, and hating herself for allowing herself to be so easily manipulated. Of course she must tell him what he wanted to hear. She must allow him to pretend that he had not hurt and discarded her, that she had quickly and easily replaced him in her life as he would do her. She must lift from his shoulders any burden of guilt or blame.

She spun away from him as he released her, not waiting to see him claimed by the blonde she could see approaching them out of the corner of her eye.

She saw them leave, though.

The brunette, with three small children, and the blonde, linking her arm through Guy's.

CHAPTER NINE

'I'M AFRAID there could be one or two complications.'

Campion stared at the specialist.

'What kind of complications?' she croaked, her rebellious stomach heaving.

It had been like this ever since Christmas, and now, on a bleak, freezing cold January day, she had just received very definite confirmation that she was pregnant.

'A vitamin deficiency—nothing that can't be put right, but I'm afraid your pregnancy won't be easy. Of course,' he looked down at his immaculate desk and then back at her, 'you could always go for a termination.'

It took several seconds for the words to sink through, but, when they did, she was horrified.

Abort Guy's baby? Never!'

'No! No, I don't want to do that.'

'No, I can see that. Well, if you're sensible,' he paused and looked hard at her, 'if you eat and rest properly . . . Of course, we'll have to monitor your progress. The baby's due in August. It's January now. You're going to have to take things very quietly for the next six weeks.' Unspoken, but there none the less, was the threat of a possible miscarriage.

Campion listened as he talked about tests and vitamins, but her mind was only half on what he was saying.

She had known before, of course, that she was pregnant, but she had not known until now how much she wanted her child. She would do anything, *anything* to protect its fragile hold on life.

'You work as a writer. Writers forget to eat, they become absorbed in what they're doing. It might be a good idea if you stopped work for the next six weeks. Do you live alone?'

Campion nodded.

'Mmm . . . Do you have any family? A friend you could stay with?'

So he didn't trust her to obey him on her own.

'No family. Some friends, but . . .'

Tactfully, he had said nothing about her baby's father, other than to ask for medical details, which she hadn't been able to supply.

'I shall be perfectly all right on my own,' she told him brightly, preparing to leave.

But would she? Her flat depressed her. A London flat was no place in which to bring up a child. A child needed a home—a proper home.

So . . . she could work just as easily outside London. She could find herself a small house somewhere.

The specialist had given her several information sheets to read. She made herself a cup of coffee—decaffeinated now, for the baby's sake—and sat down to read them.

The ring on the doorbell surprised her. She wasn't expecting any visitors. She went to answer it, surprised to see Lucy outside.

Her friend, now well into her pregnancy, really was blooming. Campion felt drained and lifeless in comparison.

'I came up to London to do some shopping. I

haven't heard from you for ages, and so I decided——' She broke off and stared at the leaflets. 'Campion, what on earth's all this stuff? My God! You're pregnant, aren't you?'

Common sense warned her to deny it, but her mind didn't seem to work very quickly these days.

Lucy sat down and stared at her. 'It's Guy's, isn't it? You're having his child. Oh, Campion, why didn't you tell me?'

Ridiculously, Campion was crying. She seemed to cry a lot these days—hormones, she supposed.

'Does he know? Have you told him? Will you tell him?'

'No, no and no again,' she sniffed. 'It was an accident, more my fault than Guy's.' She blushed when she saw the way Lucy was looking at her. 'I want this baby, Lucy,' she added quietly, not really knowing what impelled her to say the words out loud.

Lucy wasn't listening to her. She had picked up one of the information sheets, and she was reading it with a frown.

'Something's wrong, isn't it?' she demanded. 'You're not well . . .'

Campion measured her chances of deceiving her, and decided that they were too slim.

'A vitamin deficiency. The specialist says I should be all right, but I've got to give up work for six weeks, and then . . . What on earth are you doing?' she demanded, as Lucy got up and went into her bedroom. She followed her and watched as she opened cupboards and drawers.

'Lucy!' she protested.

'You're coming home with me right now. No, don't argue! I'm not leaving you here on your

own.' She turned to her, her expression unusually
fierce.

'I've lost one child, Campion. I wouldn't want
anyone to have that experience, least of all you.
Come home with me. We'll be company for one
another.'

'I . . . I can't! What will Howard say?'

'He'll be delighted. He's got to spend some time
in the States. He'll feel much happier about leaving
me if he knows I've got you for company, and we
can talk babies all day long if we feel like it. Mrs T
will be in her element with two of us to boss
around!'

She oughtn't to give in so weakly, but the
temptation was too much to resist.

'Why won't you tell Guy?' Lucy asked her when
they were both sitting in the Rolls. Paul had
expressed no surprise at being informed that
Campion was going home with them.

'He wouldn't want to know.'

'Oh, God, that insecurity complex of yours! He
wanted you, Campion. He made *love* to you.'

'No, he didn't want *me,*' Campion told her
quietly, slowly repeating what she had overheard.

'I don't believe it,' Lucy said flatly. 'Guy would
never do anything like that.'

'But he did,' Campion told her gently. 'I don't
want to talk about it. It's over, finished . . .' She
leaned back against the leather upholstery and
closed her eyes.

Seeing her exhaustion and frail hold on her self-
control, Lucy fell silent. Now wasn't the time, and
Campion hadn't the strength. Perhaps later . . .

*   *   *

Campion told Helena that she was taking a sab-batical, and that she would be in touch with her later in the year. She also told her that she had decided against entering into another contract with Adam Hart.

There were other publishers, and for now she had enough money to take care of both herself and her child comfortably for some time to come. Gradually, she was finding that she was becoming more and more self-absorbed, and more and more wrapped up in her coming child.

In March, she had a check-up. The specialist was pleased with her progress, and cautiously optimistic that the danger had been overcome.

At the end of the month, when the daffodils were budding and a cold, clean wind swept the sky, sending the clouds scudding like a busy broom, Howard came home for a brief stay.

Things were not going well with the American side of his business. He was in partnership with two Americans, and he was considering closing down that side of his operation.

On Saturday, Campion went out for a walk so that they could have some time together. She wasn't looking forward to her eventual return to London, and she was now seriously considering buying a small house in the locality. Lucy lived in a very pleasant part of the world, as yet unspoiled by any rush of London commuters. Someone a long time ago had planted the park surrounding the house with a vast profusion of bulbs, and Campion paused to admire them as she strolled towards the gates.

Her ultimate destination was the village, almost a mile away, where she had promised Lucy that she would buy bread, and where she also wanted to call on the local estate agent.

The road from the house to the village was relatively quiet, the odd car sped past her, one even slowed down and as she glanced up she had a fleeting impression of a dark haired woman and several children crammed inside the large estate car.

She was tired when she reached the village. It was surprisingly hard work, struggling against the buffeting wind.

She sat down on a wooden seat to get her breath. A group of teenagers on bicycles were chatting outside the newsagent. A woman emerged with three children in tow, and Campion stiffened as she recognised Guy's sister . . . Meg Drummond, she remembered.

This was a meeting she could not blame Lucy for.

She ducked her head instinctively, even though, as far as she knew, the other woman had no idea who she was—nor surely would want to speak to her if she did. But when she looked back, after what she judged was a suitable interval, she was horrified to see the woman walking determinedly towards her.

'I have to talk to you,' she announced without preamble. 'I know who you are. Guy pointed you out to me at the children's party. I can't . . .'

She gasped as Campion stood up hurriedly, her coat catching in the breeze and blowing open to reveal the betraying swell of her body.

'Guy was right!' She drew away from Campion, as though she were in some way contaminated. 'I didn't think he could be.' She sounded almost dazed. 'I . . . he told me not to interfere. He said you were involved with someone else.' She looked at Campion's swollen stomach and then away again, and demanded fiercely, 'Do you realise what you've done to him?'

Campion stared at her. 'What *I've* done to *him*?'

'Yes,' the other woman said bitterly. 'We used to tease him and tell him that he'd never fall in love; that he was too self-sufficient. Oh, God, how I wish that we'd been right!'

None of what she was hearing made sense. Campion turned to walk away, and gasped as cramp attacked her muscles. She couldn't move. An intense feeling of panic and fear rushed through her, and the sky seemed to fall down towards her. She blinked unsteadily, and in the distance heard a woman say huskily, 'Tom! Quick, run and get Daddy.' And then the whole world turned black, and she was sucked down into warm darkness.

When she came round, she was sitting on the bench. A man held her wrist, measuring her pulse. Meg Drummond sat beside her, watching her with anxious, guilty eyes, and three identical pairs of grey eyes stared curiously at her.

'See? She isn't dead, after all. I told you she wasn't,' the tallest said scornfully to his siblings.

'Tom, please! I'm so sorry . . . I didn't . . .'

'What my wife is trying to tell you,' the man's voice interrupted pleasantly, 'is that she wants to apologise for her impulsive outburst. How do you feel?'

'Fine, I'm fine,' Campion lied mechanically. She wanted them all to go away. She wanted to be left alone in peace, without these reminders of Guy

pressing in all around her. How like him his
nephews were . . . or was the smallest one a girl?
Hard to tell with that short hair and those jeans.
She felt muzzy and weak; the thought of the walk
back to the house made her quail.

'Mmm . . .' The man's voice was professionally
non-committal. He had to be a doctor.

'How far advanced is your pregnancy?'

'Four months.' She said it without thinking.

'Four months?' Guy's sister stared at her.
'But——' she broke off and said hurriedly to her
husband. 'Tait, I think we should give her a lift
home. She isn't in any fit state to walk.'

'Yes, I agree.' He released Campion's wrist and
smiled calmly at her. 'My wife will stay with you
while I get the car. Come on, kids.'

Her fascinated audience were obviously
reluctant to leave but, as they did so, she heard the
eldest one saying with relish, 'She'll get loads fatter
than that before she has the baby. You should have
seen Mum when she was having you . . .'

She was alone with Guy's sister. How on earth
had this happened? She had come out for a quiet
walk, that was all.

'It's Guy's baby, isn't it?'

'I thought we'd already established that,'
Campion said curtly.

The other woman frowned and then demanded,
'Why haven't you told him?'

Campion stared at her.

'According to you, he already knows. Guy was
right, you said,' she reminded her.

'Right?' Meg looked confused, and then her
mouth opened in a round 'oh' of enlightenment.
'No, you misunderstood me. Guy doesn't know

you're *pregnant*. He thinks . . . he thinks you're involved with someone else. And so did I, until I heard you say you were four months gone.'

'Someone *else*?' Campion struggled to sit up, and then sank back on to the bench, as she realised she was still too weak to support herself properly.

'How could he think that?' she began, and then flushed, remembering their brief verbal exchange at the party.

'Tait's here with the car. We can talk later. I'm Margaret, by the way, Guy's sister.'

'Yes, I know. One of the twins.'

'Yes.'

Somehow or other, room was made for Campion in the car. She was feeling dizzy again, and it was a relief to lean back and close her eyes.

It wasn't far back to the house, and with a bit of luck she might be able to make it to her room without either Mrs Timmins or Lucy guessing what had happened.

She opened her eyes. The drive seemed to be taking a long time. Alarm jolted through her as she stared at her unfamiliar surroundings.

She gripped the back of the front passenger seat and Margaret turned round.

'We're taking you home with us,' she said quickly. 'It seems best . . .'

Best? For whom? She didn't want to go home with them.

'Please, I'd rather . . .'

Margaret had turned up the radio, and either wasn't aware or didn't want to be aware of her protest. This was kidnap, Campion told herself. She could sue them—and then her stomach lurched protestingly as the car hit a dip in the road. Tait, seeing her expression in his driving mirror, increased his speed slightly.

The car turned into the drive of a modern, well built house and stopped.

'Straight upstairs, I think, Meg,' Campion heard Tait saying calmly to his wife, as he helped her out of the car.

She caught the look of mingled panic and guilt that crossed the other woman's face, and her husband's quick, negative shake of his head, and fear clutched at her

Her baby—she was going to lose her baby! She must have said it out loud, because Tait told her soothingly, 'Nothing of the kind! Four-month babies aren't that easy to lose, and if it's got the French blood in its veins . . .'

Nevertheless, he was quick to examine her once she was upstairs and, in her anxiety for her unborn child, Campion was forced to tell him about her specialist's fears.

'Don't worry. You're going to be fine. I'll ring your friends and let them know——'

'That you—I've been kidnapped,' she supplied bitterly.

'Yes. I'm sorry about that, but you see . . .'

But Campion wasn't listening. She had drifted off to sleep, exhausted by the events of the afternoon.

Downstairs, Meg asked her husband anxiously, 'Is she going to be all right? If anything happens, I'll never forgive myself.'

'You shouldn't have interfered, Meg—but yes, I think she'll be OK,' he told her, relenting when he saw her worried face.

'When I think of how angry I was! You see, I

thought she'd just turned her back on Guy, and that the baby . . .'

'Guy's a grown man, Meg. You can't run his life for him. He wouldn't thank you for interfering. You know that.'

'But it's so obvious that she loves him, and he thinks—he thinks she's involved with someone else!'

Tait had come to the same conclusion but, unlike his impetuous wife, he did not believe in interfering in the lives of others.

'I'd better go and ring her friends.'

When she came back, half an hour later, Meg looked pleased and rather bemused.

'You'll never guess what happened!' she told him. 'I couldn't believe it myself at first . . .'

'It must be far-fetched, then,' her husband agreed drily.

'Yes, very unfortunate indeed.'

Meg was disappointed. She had expected more of a reaction than that. 'Well, we're going to have to do something. You must see that.'

'No, Meg,' Tait told her firmly, adding, 'What I do see is that we have a young woman upstairs, who's four months pregnant, and who is not at all well. Any shocks at this time . . .' He saw her face fall, and said gently, 'I know you mean well, Meg, but have you thought? Guy might not be as thrilled to discover that he's going to be a father as you seem to think.'

Campion, standing in the passage outside the kitchen door, heard every word. Odd that she should feel such pain when, after all, they did nothing other than confirm everything she had thought herself.

'You mean, I mustn't tell him,' Meg said wist-fully.

'I don't think it would be very wise, or very fair, do you? If, as you say, he's already left for the States . . . He'll be there for close on two months, and then we're all flying out to Canada for the wedding.'

'But he ought to know,' she protested stubbornly.

'Meg,' he took hold of both her hands in his own, 'have you thought that there's nothing to stop Guy from getting in touch with Campion if he wishes to do so?'

'He thinks she's involved with someone else.'

There was a tiny silence, and Campion felt her heart pound.

'I know what you're trying to tell me, Tait,' she heard Meg saying shakily at last, 'but you're wrong, I know you're wrong. It's all Sandra's fault . . . I've never liked her.'

'I thought she was your best friend,' Tait responded drily.

'That was before! Tait, what are we going to do about Campion?'

'Nothing. There's nothing we *can* do,' he told her firmly. 'Both she and Guy are adults, Meg. We can't interfere.'

Very quietly, Campion went back to her room.

So, now she knew. Like her, Guy's brother-in-law believed that Guy was glad to be free of their relationship, and that he wouldn't welcome the news that she was carrying his child.

CHAPTER TEN

IT WAS two days before Campion was allowed to go back to Lucy's. Two days, during which Meg haunted her bedroom, regaling her with tales of her childhood, and Guy's care and devotion. She learned how he had sacrificed his own education, how he had left school and gone to work at eighteen. How he was the most perfect big brother that ever existed.

Meg even brought her twin sister to see her. Alison was a slightly softer version of Meg, but very obviously just as devoted to Guy.

Neither of them seemed able to understand why she could not believe that Guy would be overjoyed to learn that he was to become a father.

'He's always adored children, hasn't he, Allie?' Meg encouraged her twin.

'Always,' Alison responded loyally and promptly.

But it wasn't until the afternoon she was due to leave that Meg brought up the subject of the Christmas party.

'Your friend told me what you'd overheard,' she said uncomfortably. 'I know how it must have sounded, but you mustn't pay any attention to Sandra. She's been after Guy for years. She's frantically jealous of you. She probably made it all up.'

'I don't think so,' Campion said quietly, and the look in her eyes made Meg bite her lip and look down at the floor, and for the first time in her life curse her beloved elder brother.

April was cold and wet. Campion found a small house to rent, not far from Lucy. It was old and tiny, only two downstairs rooms, and a kitchen and two bedrooms, but it had a lovely garden with a small orchard, and already she could see the pram underneath the apple trees while she sat typing beside it.

Mrs Timmins insisted on giving the house what she termed a good 'going over' before Campion was allowed to move in.

Lucy's very superior interior designer was also called in, even though Campion protested at the expense. She had her child and its future to think about now, and she was determined that her baby would have all the security she could give it, both emotional and financial.

'You want the baby's room to be just right, don't you.' Lucy coaxed, and somehow or other Campion found herself giving way.

Her word processor was installed, and she started work on the sequel to her novel about Lynsey, her anxiety over her baby's security encouraging her, and yet she found that, far from it being a chore, she was enjoying her task. Her research into the background for the first book had equipped her with enough information to start writing the second without any delay, and she found, as the days passed, that she was creating for Lynsey and her children an almost idyllic lifestyle, filled with warmth and love . . . the kind of lifestyle she longed to be able to give her own child. There was only one difference. Lynsey's first child's arrival was an event longed for by both parents.

Guy was still in America, so Meg had told her artlessly on one of her visits. Campion was beginning to suspect that Meg was mothering her; certainly never a week went by without her phoning or calling in person and, oddly, Campion discovered that she didn't resent the other woman's concern. In fact, it gave her a feeling of warmth . . . of being almost a part of Guy's family. It was a feeling she fought against giving in to, warning herself that it would be much more sensible for her to tell Meg that she didn't want there to be any contact between them, but how could she, when Meg was her sole means of hearing about Guy? And Campion was constantly greedy for news about him, willing Meg to tell her more than the casual snippets she threw into their conversations. Guy was well . . . Guy was working hard . . . Guy wasn't planning to return for some time . . .

She knew she was only storing up trouble for herself. What would happen when the baby arrived? She could hardly continue the association then.

May was warm, buds unfurled on the apple trees and Campion succumbed to an unaccustomed feeling of contentment—until she went to London for her check-up.

'Mmm,' her specialist had said doubtfully, and 'mmm,' again.

'Is anything wrong?' Campion asked in panic when she was dressed. She had been so careful, so proud of herself for sticking to his regime, and if she were to lose Guy's baby now . . .

'Well, not exactly. I'll have to do some further

tests.'

'What is it? What's wrong?' Campion demanded anxiously.

'Nothing's wrong,' he assured her. 'I'm just getting two heartbeats.'

'*Two?*' Campion stared at him. 'You mean . . .'

'I think you're having twins.'

'Twins!' Lucy shrieked when she told her. 'My God, you don't believe in doing things by halves, do you? Of course, they run in the family, don't they? Meg and her sister Alison——' She broke off contritely as she saw Campion's face.

Afterwards, Campion realised that it must have been Lucy who told Meg Drummond, but at the time she had no idea that Meg had found out, let alone that she was in a fever of frustration.

Campion was bound to have girls, Meg's busy mind reasoned. Two girls . . . her nieces . . . she was never going to be allowed to know if Campion continued to refuse to get in touch with Guy. And yet she loved him, Meg was sure. She couldn't resist talking about him; she stayed near the Drummond house, when it would have made more sense to shun any contact with Guy's relatives. *If* she hated him . . . Well, from what Meg had heard, it seemed she had every reason to do so. What on earth had possessed Guy to leave the girl alone, without putting up any sort of fight?

But, remembering the look on her brother's face when she last saw him, Meg didn't pursue that particular thought. Guy hadn't looked like that for many years, thank God. But how long did he mean to stay away? Guy had never been a good letter writer, and during the brief telephone calls they

had received since his departure he had been curt
and abrupt, not his normal self at all. Because
work on the script wasn't going well, or because he
was missing Campion?

Meg knew that he and his author were renting a
house some way outside Hollywood but, knowing
her brother, she doubted that he would be joining
in the glamorous Californian lifestyle. He was
more likely to be working obsessively, smothering
any pain he might feel in the sheer volume of work,
just as Campion was working away at her new
book, hiding away in her latest story when real life
seemed unbearable. The latest information, that
Guy wasn't due home for some time, worried Meg.
But she couldn't do everything by herself. She
needed someone to help her.

She considered asking Tait, and then discarded
the idea; when one got down to basics, men had no
imagination. They thought in straight lines,
logically and single-mindedly. Women were
different, and something definitely had to be done.

Guy received the telegram at the end of a long, hot
Hollywood day which he had spent alternately
arguing with the film's director and placating
Julien Forbes, whose book was being used as the
basis for the film.

Julien was objecting to various changes the
director wanted to make, and, while Guy had every
sympathy with him, he was beginning to wish he
had never agreed to help. Agents were *persona non
grata* on any film set, and if he hadn't been
desperate to get away from England, and if Julien
hadn't been so insistent, he would have
recommended someone else for the job.

He knew damn well what was bugging him, Guy acknowledged derisively: a certain woman whose image he just could not get out of his mind, whose body he ached to have beside him at night when he went to bed, whose conversation he missed damnably. Campion. What was she doing? Who was she with . . . the same man who had been sharing her room in Cornwall?

When the telegram came, he thought for a moment that she had sent it. She'd decide that her freedom was worth less than what they had enjoyed together, and she'd sent for him to come to her . . .

He took the telegram from the messenger and read the simple message.

'Come home immediately. We need you,' it read, and it was signed 'Meg and Alison'.

He headed straight for the phone.

Alison had joined the Drummonds for their evening meal for the second evening in succession; Meg had insisted to her twin that she needed some moral support in case Guy arrived. A phone call to his house had elicited the fact that he was on his way to England, but they had not been able to discover when to expect him. Naturally enough, Tait was aware of his wife's and his sister-in-law's tension; the air was practically humming with it.

Both of them literally jumped in their seats when the doorbell rang, and Meg went pea-green when Tait got up and said calmly, 'Stay here, I'll answer it.'

He was looking anything but calm when he walked into the dining-room five minutes later, an exhausted, unshaven Guy at his side.

As she looked at her brother, Meg felt a pang of remorse. He looked dreadful—pale and tired, but, more than that, almost haunted.

They had almost finished their meal, and after one look at his wife's guilty face, Tait said succinctly, 'Right, kids, out.' He waited until the door had closed behind them before saying, 'All right, Meg. What's going on?'

Meg looked appealingly at Alison, but her twin could only shake her head. She had gone as pale as Guy, and, looking at her stricken face, Meg knew that there was only one person who was going to be able to go through with their plan, and that was herself.

She cleared her throat, alarmed to discover that the look in Guy's eyes made her feel about five years old.

There was only one way she was going to be able to do this . . . It was too late for tact or diplomacy. She took a deep breath, and Tait warned her, 'Meg, you've brought Guy rushing half-way across the world in the belief that the family's suffered some kind of tragedy. I think you owe it to him to tell him why, don't you?'

Meg discovered for the first time in her life that she was actually frightened of her brother. Gone was the indulgence, the tenderness she had always known, and in its place was a hard, unyielding anger.

'Guy, it's Campion . . . Campion Roberts.' She gulped nervously. 'She . . . she's having a baby . . .'

Just for a fraction of time she saw the shock and anguish in his eyes, and then it was gone, leaving them flat and cold.

'And you've brought me God knows how many

thousand miles to tell me that a woman I haven't seen in months is pregnant. Why, for God's sake?'

He didn't know! He really didn't know, Meg realised, and if it hadn't been for that illuminating moment of betrayal when she had seen the truth in his eyes, she couldn't have gone on.

Underneath the table, she groped for Alison's hand and, holding it tightly, she said huskily, 'The baby . . . babies are yours.'

There was an electric, humming silence, which Tait broke by saying dazedly, 'Meg . . .'

But no one was listening to him. Guy stood up and gripped Meg's arm, bruising it without realising what he was doing, his face white and strained beneath the Hollywood tan, and two days' stubble.

'Say that again,' he demanded thickly.

Meg lifted her head and looked into his eyes, her heartbeat slowing back to normal. It was going to be all right . . . She had been right. He *did* care.

'Campion is carrying your child . . . children,' she amended, with a brief smile. 'She's having twins.'

She reached out and touched him then, her eyes soft and pleading.

'Guy, she loves you so much. What happened between you . . . Every time I see her, she asks me about you, even though I can see she's trying desperately not to. Those poor little babies . . . Our nieces!' she added. 'We had to make you come home, you must see that,' she persisted when he made no reply. He looked, in fact, as though he had stopped listening to her, an arrested expression, which she had no difficulty in recognising at all, lightening his eyes.

'Couldn't you have chosen a less drastic method?' he asked drily, but the anger had gone from his face and body, and he was even beginning to smile slightly.

'Such as what? Meg demanded rallyingly. 'Come home—Campion is pregnant?' She shook her head and clung to his arm, demanding, 'Oh, Guy, you do love her, don't you? I was so sure you must, and I wanted desperately to tell her. She looked so forlorn, so . . . unhappy, but I dared not, just in case I was wrong. And then, after her fall——' she added artlessly, ignoring the warning look her husband gave her.

'Her fall! *What* fall?' Guy demanded. 'Is she all right? Is she . . .'

'Guy, she's fine,' Tait told him calmly. 'She fainted rather badly some time ago, but since then she's been fine. At least, physically.'

'She misses you dreadfully,' Meg intervened.

'That's enough, Meg.' Tait told her crisply. 'I don't think Campion would be too happy if she knew you were betraying her confidences like this . . .'

She turned from her husband to her brother and demanded 'Guy, what are you going to do?'

'That, my dear wife, is none of your business,' Tait told her firmly.

Campion couldn't remember such a perfect day. The sun shone, the air was balmy, bees hummed in the long grass she was too lazy to cut. The house was hers and, despite all her protests, she loved its pastel-washed walls and soft chintzes. And the nursery. She smiled and patted the mound of her stomach. Two and a half more months, and she could quite easily spend them all here in the orchard, lazing in the sun.

Nature had given her a gift she had not expected, over and above her two unborn children. She had given her peace . . . sanctuary from her heartache, a breathing space in which normal emotions were suspended to allow her to concentrate solely on the new lives she carried.

Above her, high in the sky, a plane droned. She closed her eyes, lulled to sleep by the sound. She slept a lot these days. A sign of depression, an inner voice nagged, but she didn't listen to it. She stretched out the blanket and sighed softly.

It was the shadow coming between her and the warmth of the sun that woke her. She looked up and saw the shape of a man; the sun dazzled her eyes, and she struggled clumsily into a sitting position.

'Guy . . .'

'Why in God's name didn't you tell me?'

No preamble, no skirting round the subject, just that fierce, angry question.

It threw her off guard, making it impossible for her to pretend she didn't know what he meant.

He was dressed in a suit, and he looked hot and uncomfortable, but his skin was tanned. A legacy from his stay in the States? As he looked at her, he tugged at his tie and released the top buttons of his shirt.

A familiar sensation curled through her body. Desperately she looked away from him. She didn't want to feel like this, to want him, to love him . . .

'How did you know?'

'Meg,' he told her tautly, his nostrils flaring

slightly as he bit out, 'God, can you *imagine* how I felt, learning that you were carrying my . . . children, right out of the blue, when I thought . . .'

'It must have been a shock,' Campion agreed coolly. She was feeling slightly dizzy, probably because she had been lying in the sun. She tried to stand up, and winced as she felt the pins and needles attack her ankle.

'What's wrong?' Guy demanded sharply, dropping to the ground beside her. One hand touched her shoulder, the other her foot. She could smell the hot male scent of him, and it made her catch her breath, bringing back memories of what it had been like to be able to touch him, to caress him.

'Campion!' His voice was roughly urgent, forcing her to look into her eyes. They were dark and strained. 'Why . . . why didn't you say something?'

His hand moved from her foot to her stomach, splaying across its swollen bulge. She was only wearing a thin cotton dress, and the heat from his skin was so intimate that she might have been naked. She felt the twins move, and in other circumstances she might almost have laughed at the expression on his face as one of them kicked hard against his palm. Dark red patches of colour burned high up on his cheekbones. He released her immediately, and she tried to quell her instinctive feeling of rejection.

'What was there to say?' she said in answer to his question. 'You'd made it plain that our relationship was over.'

'I . . . I *what*? What the hell are you talking about? I *loved* you. I thought I'd made that more than clear.' He shook his head, as though he couldn't grasp what she was saying. 'I loved you, but I didn't want to trap you into a commitment given in a haze of sexual ecstasy.' She saw him grimace. 'I wanted to give you time . . . time to experiment a little, to find yourself, to explore your sexuality. I told myself that, if you did love me, I had nothing to lose, and that, if you didn't, trying to tie you to me wouldn't work anyway. I didn't want to treat you like Craig did.'

'You loved me?' Campion couldn't believe it. 'You're lying! You took me to bed, as part of your job as my agent.'

'So that you would re-write the book? How dare you believe that, after what we had together? How could you credit such arrant nonsense with any shred of reality?'

He had taken hold of her and was practically shaking her. He was furious with her, Campion recognised.

'When we got back from Wales, you walked away from me without a word,' she challenged bitterly. 'All that week I was away, I kept hoping you'd ring me.'

'I did better than that. I went to see you. I'd driven all evening to get there. God, I'd missed you so much! I couldn't stay away any longer. I had to tell you how I felt, whether you were ready to hear it or not. I got the number of your room from reception.

'I suppose I was pretty arrogant. I was sure you'd welcome me with open arms, so sure that I didn't say a word to you about my plans to visit you on tour. I simply turned up, because I wanted to surprise you . . . wanted to see pleasure in your

eyes when you looked at me. Only it didn't work
out that way, did it?'

She stared at him, stunned by the bitterness in
his voice.

'I went upstairs . . . you were just going inside
your room. There was a man with you——'

'A man?' Suddenly, she remembered. 'It was
you,' she said huskily. 'The man we thought had
got the wrong floor. I wasn't well—Antony was
helping me to my room. I barely knew him!'

His jaw tensed. 'At Christmas, when I tried to
talk to you, you told me there was someone else.'

'I lied. I'd just heard . . .'

'Yes, I know what you'd just heard,' he interrupted tersely. 'Meg and Alison have been filling
me in. It seemed that they didn't want to lose you
any more than I did. God, I could shake you until
your teeth rattle! How could you think . . .?' He
shook his head suddenly, looking suddenly
unutterably weary and vulnerable. Campion
caught hold of his sleeve.

'I was so insecure, Guy. What we had was so
new, so precious, I couldn't . . .'

'Trust me?' he asked bitterly.

'No. Trust *myself,* my judgement. I'd been
wrong once——'

'Yes, when you were nineteen . . . a child.' He
took hold of her face, and she saw the muscle
clench in his jaw as he looked at her. 'I knew from
the first I loved you, but what I didn't bargain for
was how much that love was going to disrupt my
life. I thought I could pretend that my work was
still important when I couldn't see you each day. I
thought I had the strength to go away and stay
away when I realised you didn't want me. I even

thought I had the strength to let you make your own choices instead of putting pressure on you, but here I am . . . ready to beg.

'I've spent weeks in Hollywood, just wanting to get on the next plane home and take you in my arms. Have you any idea what I've been through these last few months, or how I felt when my sister blurted out that you were carrying my child . . . children?' he amended huskily. 'Why didn't you tell me?'

'Because I was frightened,' she told him simply. 'I didn't see how someone like you could possibly want me, and I was afraid of being hurt again.'

He didn't answer her in words, but the expression in his eyes made her look away.

'Tait says you haven't been well.' He was searching her face as he spoke. 'You fainted.'

'It wasn't important,' she reassured him. 'I'm all right now.'

'How all right? Well enough to get married?'

'Married?' She felt her pulse jerk under his fingers where they circled her wrist.

'We're a little old-fashioned about these things in my family,' he told her drily. 'Meg tells me she's never going to speak to me again if I do her out of her nieces.'

'Nieces?' Campion's eyebrows rose.

'Oh, Meg has a thing about little girls. She's convinced that she and Tait will only produce boys, and she seems to be right. She's equally convinced that you and I are going to produce girls, this time round, at least . . .'

'And is that why you want to marry me? Because Meg doesn't want to be deprived of her nieces?'

'No, it isn't,' he told her softly. 'It's because I

don't want to be deprived of the woman I love, or the children she's going to give me,' he added, putting his hand on her stomach.

Pleasure quivered through her, and as though she had spoken it out aloud he muttered thickly, 'Campion! God, how I've missed you.'

And then he was kissing her, fiercely, hungrily, letting her see how wrong she had been, and how much, how very much he did need her.

It was a long time before he released her.

'I've come straight here from the airport,' he told her as they walked into the house. 'Do you suppose I could beg a bed for the night?'

'There's only mine . . .'

They stopped walking, and she quivered as he drew her towards him.

'And it's not very big,' she tried to say, but his mouth was muffling the words, and anyway she didn't think she cared how large or small the bed was, just as long as they could share it.

'Should we be doing this?' Guy asked with sensual contentment several hours later.

The evening sun poured in through the open windows, gliding their bodies, his dark and lean, hers pale and swollen with the burden of the new life she carried.

'I don't see why not.' Campion wriggled closer to him, her breath catching as his hand lazily caressed her breast, sensitive now in the later stages of her pregnancy.

There had been a brief moment when she had felt uncomfortably aware of her pregnancy and her clumsiness, but Guy had soon dispelled it, telling her and showing her how erotic he found her changed shape.

His mouth replaced his fingers and she sighed rapturously as he tugged gently on her nipple.

His hand lay splayed across her belly, and when he released her, abruptly lifting his head from her breast, she looked at him in concern, until he made her gurgle with laughter by saying in awe, 'My God, we've got an audience. One of them kicked me!'

'Serves you right for poaching on their preserves,' Campion teased him.

They were married at the end of the mouth, with Guy's mother still looking rather surprised to discover that her eldest son was soon to make her a grandmother. They were going to look for a house in Dorset, but not until after the babies were born. Until then, they would live in Campion's small cottage.

'I know why you don't want to move,' Campion teased him mischievously, after the wedding was over and they were alone. They had elected not to go away. Why should they? They had all the privacy they needed right here at the cottage. 'You're getting to like this small bed.'

'Mmm—and it's getting smaller by the day,' Guy complained. 'It wasn't even designed for two, never mind four . . .'

The twins arrived safely at the end of August. Guy stayed with Campion throughout the birth.

'I'd better go and ring Meg,' he told her wryly, glancing down into the small bundles nestled in his wife's arms.

His brother-in-law answered the phone.

'Twin girls, I knew it!' Meg crowed when Tait replaced the receiver. 'Two adorable little girls. I can see them now, dressed in pink.'

'Er—no—not girls.'

'Not girls?' Meg glanced sharply at him. 'You mean——'

'Boys,' Tait told her gravely. 'Twin boys. But don't worry, Guy said he'd do his best for girls next time.' He grinned at his wife. 'You know what I think?'

'No, and I don't want to, either,' Meg said crossly.

'Mmm—pity. My aunt Jane had three boys, you know, and then on the fourth attempt—bingo!'

'A girl?' Meg breathed, perking up.

'Triplets,' Tait told her solemnly, ducking as Meg threw a cushion at him.

'Well, you never know . . . It might work. Worth having a try . . .'

'Tait Drummond' she warned him direfully. 'If we have another boy . . .'

In the hospital, Campion waited for Guy to rejoin her.

'Told Meg the bad news?' she asked with a smile.

'Not Meg! I'm not that brave. I spoke to Tait instead.' He caught hold of her hand. 'Happy?'

'Blissfully,' Campion assured him. 'More than I ever imagined possible. 'She frowned, and then said thoughtfully, 'Guy . . . as my agent, what would you think about me writing a sequel to my book, telling the story of Dickon and Lynsey's children?'

'I think that's a very good idea . . . But as your

husband, I don't give a damn. I love you, Mrs French,' he murmured against her mouth. 'Have I told you that?'

'Yes, but you can tell me again—I'll never get tired of hearing you say it,' Campion whispered back.

Coming in June…

Harlequin Presents…

PENNY JORDAN

a reason for being

We invite you to join us in celebrating Harlequin's
40th Anniversary with this very special book we
selected to publish worldwide.

While you read this story, millions of women in 100
countries will be reading it, too.

A Reason for Being by Penny Jordan is being
published in June in the Presents series in 19
languages around the world. Join women around
the world in helping us to celebrate 40 years of
romance.

Penny Jordan's *A Reason for Being* is Presents June
title #1180. Look for it wherever paperbacks are
sold.

PENNY-1

You'll flip . . . your pages won't!
Read paperbacks *hands-free* with

Book Mate · I

The perfect "mate" for all your romance paperbacks

Traveling • Vacationing • At Work • In Bed • Studying
• Cooking • Eating

Perfect size for all standard paperbacks, this wonderful invention makes reading a pure pleasure! Ingenious design holds paperback books OPEN and FLAT so even wind can't ruffle pages — leaves your hands free to do other things. Reinforced, wipe-clean vinyl-covered holder flexes to let you turn pages without undoing the strap . . . supports paperbacks so well, they have the strength of hardcovers!

SEE-THROUGH STRAP

Pages turn WITHOUT opening the strap.

Reinforced back stays flat.

Built in bookmark.

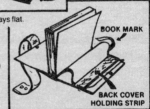

BOOK MARK

BACK COVER HOLDING STRIP

10" x 7¼", opened.
Snaps closed for easy carrying, too.

Available now. Send your name, address, and zip code, along with a check or money order for just $5.95 + .75¢ for postage & handling (for a total of $6.70) payable to Reader Service:

      Reader Service
      Bookmate Offer
      901 Fuhrmann Blvd.
      P.O. Box 1396
      Buffalo, N.Y. 14269-1396

Offer not available in Canada
*New York and Iowa residents add appropriate sales tax.

BM-G

"NEW"

Harlequin Historicals

*Storytelling at its best
by some of your favorite authors such as
Kristen James, Nora Roberts, Cassie Edwards*

Strong, independent heroines
Heroes you'll fall in love with
Compelling love stories

History has never been so romantic.

Look for them now wherever Harlequin Books are sold.

HIST-L-1RR

COMING IN JUNE

Janet
DAILEY

THE MASTER FIDDLER

Jacqui didn't want to go back to college, and she didn't
want to go home. Tombstone, Arizona, wasn't in her
plans, either, until she found herself stuck there en route
to L.A. after ramming her car into rancher Choya Barnett's
Jeep. Things got worse when she lost her wallet and
couldn't pay for the repairs. The mechanic wasn't
interested when she practically propositioned him to get
her car back—but Choya was. He took care of her bills and
then waited for the debt to be paid with the only thing
Jacqui had to offer—her virtue.

Watch for this bestselling Janet Dailey favorite, coming in
June from Harlequin.

Also watch for *Something Extra* in August and *Sweet
Promise* in October.

JAN-MAS-1